PONY CLUB SECRETS

stardust and the Daredevil Ponies

D0030290

PONY CLUB SECRETS

Stardust and the Daredevil Ponies

STACY GREGG

HarperCollins *Children's Books*

N

CASTLE CHASE LOCATION

ANGELIQUE'S TRAILER

RUPERT'S TRAILER

COSTUME TRAILER

MAKE-UP TRAILER

DINING HALL

VAMPIRE RIDERS' BARRACKS

LIGHTING & PROP'S DEPARTMENT

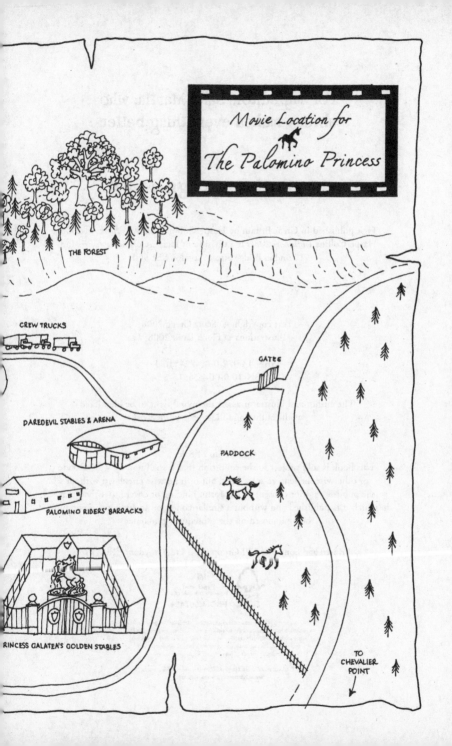

For my editor, Sally Martin, who
always makes everything better

www.stacygregg.co.uk

First published in Great Britain by HarperCollins *Children's Books* in 2008.
HarperCollins *Children's Books* is a division of HarperCollins*Publishers* Ltd,
1 London Bridge Street, London SE1 9GF

ISBN-13 978-0-00-724516-1
ISBN-10 0-00-724516-5

Printed and bound by CPI Group (UK) Ltd, Croydon, CR0 4YY

MIX
Paper from
responsible sources
FSC® C007454

Chapter 1

The dark castle gleamed in the rain, its stone turrets like blackened teeth against the moon. It had seen many storms like this one. Perched high on top of a rocky citadel, it was at the mercy of such grim weather. As the rain fell like a cloak, the huge iron portcullis that hung over the drawbridge creaked and groaned in the wind. A wolf howled at the cold moon. Then, louder than either of these, came another sound – the thunder of hoofbeats.

Far below the castle, at the foot of the mountain fortress, a horse and rider could be seen in the moonlight. The rider was a young woman with long blonde hair. She wore pale blue jodhpurs and her white cotton blouse was soaked from the lashing rain. The horse she was riding was impossibly beautiful, a golden palomino with a mane and tail so white they almost sparkled in the pale light.

The palomino's hooves flashed and clattered against the cobbled stones of the mountain path as the girl drove the horse on, up and up the terraced steps which wound like a corkscrew around the mountainside to the castle above.

As the girl and the horse galloped up to reach the second terrace it suddenly became clear that they were not alone. Seven riders on jet-black horses were quickly closing in on them. The riders looked enormous compared to the girl. They wore long black robes that billowed out behind them as they rode. Black hoods hid their faces, making them look like ghostly apparitions in the dark night.

The hooded horsemen were gaining on the girl and by the time she reached the third terrace they had surrounded her. Trapped, the palomino turned on the horsemen and reared in the air, lashing out with her front hooves, catching one of the black-robed riders with a glancing blow to the shoulder.

The hooded rider grabbed at his injured shoulder and cursed the palomino in a strange language. Then he gave instructions to the other horsemen and they obeyed him without question, forming a tight half-circle around the palomino. As the horses closed in, the palomino began snorting and stamping, turning this way and that, looking for a way to escape.

Up close, the black horses were monstrous and otherworldly. Their eyes gleamed red, their mouths frothed as they champed at their bits and their bridles were strung with strange talismen, carved symbols that hinted at the power of the ancient curse that bound them to their fate.

Suddenly the head horseman rode forward to face the girl. The other riders closed ranks behind him and stood, watching and waiting as their leader raised his pale, bony hand and drew back the hood of his cape.

The face that was revealed beneath the hood did not belong to any earthly man. The horseman had no hair at all and his bald head throbbed with pale, purplish-grey veins. His cruel, pale eyes and hooked nose gave him a crow-like appearance. His skin, which shone horribly in the moonlight, was as white as a corpse.

The palomino snorted in fear at the sight of him and the girl put her hand to the sword that lay on her hip, ready to unsheathe it.

"Leave her alone, Francis," the girl said bravely. "You cannot possibly think you will win like this."

"Oh, but that is exactly what I think, Princess," the black-robed rider hissed like a lizard. "Tonight we take Seraphine's life. She is the last of her kind. Your last hope. When she joins us and becomes one of the Horses of Darkness then you will have lost your kingdom forever."

The horseman jumped down from his black mount and stepped forward so that he was standing before the palomino. A smile played across his lips, which widened to reveal a set of long white fangs.

"Say good night, Seraphine," the vampire rider said softly as he opened his mouth wide and lunged forward to plunge his fangs deep into the palomino's golden neck...

"And... cut!" a voice shouted out. The rain suddenly stopped and the studio lights flashed on, bathing everyone in a golden glow.

"Terrific! Great scene, everyone! That's a wrap!"

There was a clapping and a whooping from the film crew at the news that the night's shooting was over. Issie jumped down off the palomino and looked up at the man who had shouted "cut!" He was sitting on an enormous camera crane erected high above the horses. "Hey, Rupert," she called out to the director, "is it all right if I take this off now?" She gestured to the long blonde wig that she was wearing over her own long dark hair.

"Absolutely. Hand it over to Helen in make-up and give your costume back to Amber, then get those horses back to the stables and you can go home. You did great work this evening, Isadora. You too, Aidan!"

The head vampire rider smiled at this, then stuck his fingers in his mouth to pull out a pair of shiny, white fake fangs. "What a relief to finally have those out! They're murder to wear when you're riding!" he said, smiling at Issie.

"Ohmygod, Aidan! You are so scary with those fangs; sometimes I almost forget that we're just making a movie and get all freaked out!" Issie grinned back.

Aidan, who was busy peeling off his latex bald cap to reveal the thick black hair hidden underneath, looked pleased at this. "Really? Thanks! You did some great stunt riding tonight, Issie. See you tomorrow on the set for breakfast, OK?"

"See you then," Issie beamed.

As Aidan set off back down the hill, leading his horse, Issie's best friends, Stella and Kate, rushed forward to help the black riders, each of them taking the reins of a pair of horses. With the lights on it was easy to see that these black horses weren't evil or strange at all, but perfectly normal horses dressed up in costume. The girls held the horses still and waited patiently as make-up artists clustered around to wipe the fake froth from the horses' mouths and remove the red glitter from around their eyes.

"That was so exciting!" Stella called out to Issie. "You did the best rear. Stardust wasn't naughty at all!"

Issie looked at the palomino mare standing next to her. "She was good, wasn't she?" Issie grinned.

"Good? She was brilliant!" Kate said, reaching forward to pat Stardust on her velvety nose. "I think you're finally getting through to her, Issie."

"I hope you're right, Kate, I really do," Issie said.

Stardust, the beautiful palomino mare, was the star of this movie and it was Issie's job as her stunt rider to make her perform for the cameras. But the mare seemed determined to misbehave and her naughty stunts had the whole film crew upset. Aunt Hester had been driven to despair by her dangerous tricks. It was Hester, of course, who was responsible for involving Issie and her friends in the whole movie business in the first place...

Issie hadn't heard from her aunt in months, since her last visit to Blackthorn Farm, so the phone call came as a bit of a surprise.

"Isadora! My favourite niece!" Hester had trilled down the phone. Her greeting made Issie laugh straightaway – Hester always called Issie her "favourite niece", when in fact she was her only niece so she didn't have much competition!

"Hi, Aunty Hess. How are things at the farm?"

Blackthorn Farm was a grand old country manor with hundreds of hectares of land, high in the hills outside Gisborne on the East Coast. It was there that Aunt Hester trained her mad menagerie of movie animals, including a team of stunt horses.

"Busy, busy, busy!" Hester told her. "We've got a big movie coming up – *The Palomino Princess* – have you heard of it?"

"Ohmygod!" Issie squealed. "Aunty Hess! I love that book! Are they making a film of it? How cool! And your horses are going to be in it?"

"Absolutely," Hester said. "Well, at least a few of them are – Paris and Nicole and Destiny and Diablo to be exact. They need quite a few stunt horses for the film, but as you'll know if you've already read the books, the

Horses of Darkness all need to be pitch black – plus we need five palominos for Galatea and her princesses. Paris and Nicole are perfect for princess horses and Diablo is having his piebald patches dyed so that he can play one of the black horses."

"That's so exciting!" Issie said.

"I'm glad you think so, dear," Hester said, "because I was hoping you might want to come and work with me on the movie."

"What? Me?"

"Well, yes. And your friends too. They're looking for riders and wranglers right now and you've got some school holidays coming up. I thought the timing was perfect," Hester said.

"I couldn't…" Issie began to protest, but Hester interrupted.

"I know Blaze is expecting her foal and you won't want to leave her alone," Hester said, "but the movie set isn't far away from Chevalier Point. You could still go home at weekends to check on her. How long is it now until she's due?"

"The vet says she has maybe a month to go," Issie said.

"Well, that's perfect then! They're doing most of the filming with the actors back at the studio on blue screen

– lots of special effects. That means the outdoor shooting at Chevalier Point is only scheduled to take a few weeks. Filming should be wrapped by the time your foal arrives."

"But I…" Issie began.

"The best part is that this will give you a chance to ride in your holidays. I mean, you can't possibly ride Blaze, can you? She must be so fat now, you won't be able to fit a girth around that tummy of hers!" Hester insisted. "Listen, my favourite niece, I could really do with your help. There are nearly two dozen horses in this film and Aidan and I are responsible for all of them. Which is fine except it's tricky to find riders who are the right size to play the palomino princesses. We need four girls who fit the costumes to double for the stars of the film, and they must be good riders. There's no problem finding stunt doubles for the black horsemen – we've got seven stunt riders who are all over six feet tall. But it's been a nightmare finding our four girls. They can't be too grown-up; Princess Galatea and her riders are all, well, actually they're about your size…" Hester paused. "We'll pay you all of course – film rates for stunt riders are really very good."

"It all sounds great, Aunty Hess!" Issie said. "And I'm sure Stella and Kate will be keen and we can find a fourth girl to ride with us…"

"Excellent!" Hester said. "So what's the best way to organise this? Do you want to put your mother on the phone? I think she's more likely to say yes if I ask her, don't you?"

"Actually, Aunty Hess, I wouldn't bet on it. She's still mad at you after last time," Issie said.

"Oh, I was hoping she would have forgotten about that by now."

The last time Issie had stayed with her aunt she had caught and ridden Destiny, a wild stallion that led a herd of wild ponies at Blackthorn Farm. Issie had returned home from her adventures with her arm in a sling – a fact that her mother was none too happy about.

"Your mum is such a fusspot," Hester sighed. "It was only a little sprain. Put her on the phone. I'm sure she'll say yes once I talk her round."

"Muuum!" Issie called with her hand over the receiver. "It's for you!"

As Mrs Brown took the phone out of her daughter's hands with a quizzical look, Issie held her breath and hoped Aunt Hester would be able to make her mother say yes.

Issie's mum and Aunt Hester were sisters, but the two women were the complete opposite of each other in every way. Hester was, as her mum put it, a "bit too bohemian for her own good". She had been an actress before she gave up the movies herself and started training animals to act instead. She had curly blonde hair that tumbled over her shoulders and always wore lots of jewellery and scarves, even when she was riding. Hester had been married three times – "All of them wonderful weddings!" as she told Issie – but she had no children of her own.

Issie's mum had only been married once – to Issie's dad – although they split up years ago and Issie hardly ever saw him. And Mrs Brown looked nothing like Hester – she looked just like Issie, with long, straight dark hair and tanned olive skin.

The most important difference between the two sisters though, as far as Issie was concerned, was horses.

Aunt Hester was horsy through and through. Right now she had twelve horses in her stables at Blackthorn Farm. Issie's mum, on the other hand, didn't like horses one bit. Issie had to beg and plead for years before her mum finally caved in and bought Mystic for her.

Issie could hear her mum on the phone now with Aunty Hess and it sounded like Hester was getting a telling-off. She could only catch snippets of the conversation but it clearly wasn't going well.

"You must be joking!" she heard her mum say. "…Yes, Hester, I know she's an excellent rider but she's also my daughter and after last time…"

Issie slunk away to the kitchen and waited for her mum to finish yelling at Hester and get off the phone. Finally, she heard the receiver being hung up and Mrs Brown appeared in the kitchen doorway, her arms crossed and her brow furrowed in a deep frown.

"I have a feeling that you already know what that phone call was about," she said.

"Uh-huh," Issie said.

"So you really want to help Hess with this movie?"

"Uh-huh."

Mrs Brown sighed. "I've told Hester that if I see so much as a sticky plaster on you when you come home this time I will hold her responsible. She insists that it's perfectly safe. There's a bit of riding apparently, but you'll mostly just be grooming the horses and mucking out the stalls."

"Wait a minute!" Issie said. "Does that mean you're going to let me go?"

Mrs Brown nodded. "Your Aunty Hess is very

convincing. You start work as a stunt rider on *The Palomino Princess* next Monday."

Issie whooped with delight. "Thanks, Mum! I'll be fine, honestly. Wow! This is so cool! I'm going straight over to see Stella. I'm sure her mum will say she can do it too! And Kate! Oh, this is going to be great!"

"Hey, hey wait!" said Mrs Brown as Issie tore off towards the front door. "Kate and Stella make three. Hester told me she needs four girl riders. She's relying on you to find her a fourth girl." Mrs Brown gave Issie a cheeky grin. "You know, I can think of one girl who would love to work on a film like this."

"Oh, very funny, Mum! I know exactly who you mean and don't you dare say her name. Don't even think it!" Issie groaned. "I'm sure we can find someone else. I'm not that desperate."

Her mum might think it was funny to lumber Issie with Natasha Tucker for the holidays but Issie couldn't think of anyone, or anything, worse. Mrs Brown didn't understand why Issie didn't like Natasha. After all, the girls were the same age – thirteen – and they were both members of the Chevalier Point Pony Club. But Natasha had it in for Issie and she was such a snob.

No, there had to be someone else that Issie could ask. There was no way she was asking awful Stuck-up Tucker. It was never going to happen. No matter what. Not in a million years.

Chapter 2

Stella's cheeks were as red as her hair. She looked like she was about to explode.

"You've done what?" she spluttered in disbelief.

"I've asked Natasha Tucker," Issie groaned.

"But why, Issie? It was going to be such fun – you, me and Kate. Why would you ask Natasha?"

"Because Aunty Hess really needed a fourth rider and it had to be a girl because we'll be stunt-doubling for the actresses in the film. Natasha is a good rider and she was the only other person I could think of."

"What about Morgan?" Kate offered. "Couldn't you have asked her instead?"

"She's away on the showjumping circuit right now with her mum," Issie said.

"This is a nightmare!" Stella fumed.

"I can't believe Natasha wants to come with us," Kate said. "She usually ignores us at pony club."

Issie shrugged. "I know." She had dreaded turning up at the River Paddock this morning to break the news to Kate and Stella. She knew they would take it badly.

"What a nightmare!" Stella groaned again.

"Oh, Stella, get over it. Don't be such a drama queen," Kate snapped.

"Natasha will have to behave herself," Issie pointed out. "Aunty Hess will be there running things and so will Aidan…"

"Aidan?" Stella said. "Ohmygod, Issie! You didn't tell me Aidan was going to be there. You haven't seen him since last summer."

"Yes, Stella, I know. I don't need reminding," Issie replied, trying to shut Stella up.

Aidan was Aunt Hester's stable manager. The last time Issie saw him was the morning they left Blackthorn Farm. She still remembered Aidan's kiss, the way his long dark fringe had brushed against her face and she had felt her heart race. She had been so shocked that she hadn't known what to say. Then Aidan had got all embarrassed and run off and they hadn't spoken since.

Only Stella and Kate knew about this – she had told them once they got home. Although Issie was beginning to wish she hadn't said anything about it to Stella at all. Stella was her best friend but she was also boy-mad and could be a bit of a twit sometimes – she was bound to blab to Aidan and embarrass her!

"Don't say anything to him about it, OK, Stella?" Issie begged her.

Stella grinned back. "About what?"

Issie blushed. "Anyway," she said, changing the subject back to Natasha, "I've already asked Natasha. Her mum says it's OK and she's coming and that's final. You need to be at my house tomorrow morning at 7 a.m. We're all trucking out to the film set together.

"How far is it?" Kate asked.

"It's only about an hour away, up past the lake," Issie said. "You know where the ruins of Chevalier Castle are, on that big hill? Well, that's why they're filming here. They're using the castle as part of their film set and they've built all these other sets and everything there. There are sleeping quarters for the stunt riders and wranglers too. We'll be working long hours and we need to take care of the horses so we'll stay there during the week, but we can come home at weekends."

"What about Blaze?" Kate asked. "You can't leave her here alone all week with the foal coming."

"I've already moved her to Winterflood Farm," Issie said. "Avery says he'll keep an eye on her. Besides, the vet says she's still not due for another month…"

"It's so exciting!" Stella blurted out. "I can't believe Blaze is actually going to have a foal!"

Issie still couldn't believe it herself. When the vet at Blackthorn Farm had told her the news she had been in shock. At first, Issie had assumed that the father must be the jet black wild stallion Destiny. Destiny had amazing bloodlines. He had been sired by Aunt Hester's own beloved Swedish Warmblood stallion, Avignon, so Issie had been very excited at the prospect of Blaze carrying the black stallion's foal.

Then, when Issie got home and her own vet examined Blaze, he dropped a bombshell. Blaze wasn't just a little bit pregnant. It seemed she was very pregnant indeed. The mare was more than three months gone already! That meant that Destiny couldn't possibly be the sire. Issie had been stunned. If Destiny wasn't the father of this foal, then who was? Finally, she figured it out. Marius! The great, grey Lipizzaner stallion was the star of the El Caballo Danza Magnifico

24

– the famed Spanish dancing horses. Blaze had once belonged to the troupe too, one of the El Caballo's seven Anglo-Arab mares, renowned for their beauty and balletic performances in the arena.

When Issie thought about it the timing made perfect sense. Blaze had been returned briefly to Francoise D'arth, the head trainer at the El Caballo Danza Magnifico. Issie remembered going to visit Blaze at the El Caballo stables. She had arrived to find Francoise busily ticking off the stable boys for allowing Marius to jump out of his paddock in with the mares. It took almost all day before the stable boys realised the stallion was in the wrong paddock.

Issie had immediately sent a letter to Francoise, telling her the exciting news, but she hadn't had a reply. Then Issie saw a big story in *PONY Magazine* about the El Caballo Danza Magnifico which said the troupe was still on its world tour. Perhaps Francoise hadn't been home and had never received Issie's letter. The French trainer would surely have got in touch if she knew that Blaze was going to have a foal.

There was still a month to go, but every day that Issie checked on Blaze she seemed to be more and more enormous. Her belly was now so huge that Issie couldn't fit a girth around her and the pony was eating twice as much hard feed as usual, as well as the lush spring grass in her paddock at Winterflood Farm.

Avery, meanwhile, was like an expectant father, fussing over the mare. He had set up the barn ready for the birth and organised the foaling monitor that would alert them the minute Blaze went into labour.

"The foaling monitor means we can leave her outdoors to graze naturally until she actually goes into labour. After that, things tend to happen very quickly," Avery warned Issie. "When my great showjumping mare Starlight was foaling, I popped off to grab a cup of tea and by the time I came back from the kitchen she'd had him and the little tyke was already trying to stand up!"

Everything was prepared and the vet had pronounced Blaze perfectly healthy. Still, Issie was nervous about going away with Aunt Hester and leaving her pony.

"She'll be fine," Avery reassured Issie. "You go and have fun. I'll keep an eye on her, don't you worry. You're only an hour away – I'll let you know the minute anything happens, I promise."

"Just don't make any cups of tea while I'm gone. I don't want Blaze to have her foal without me!" Issie had joked.

Even with Avery's reassurances, Issie didn't want to say

goodbye to Blaze. On the night before the truck was due to pick them up and take them to the film set, she stopped by Winterflood Farm and stood in the paddock for ages, giving the mare snuggles and feeding her at least six carrots.

"After all," she giggled as Blaze snuffled and munched a carrot from the palm of her hand, "you are eating for two, aren't you, girl?"

She ran her hands one last time through Blaze's long flaxen-blonde mane. The mare was so pretty with her dished Arabian face and her perfect white blaze. Issie loved Blaze so deeply now it seemed strange when she thought back to the day they first met.

It was Tom Avery who had brought Blaze to her. The chestnut Anglo-Arab had been so awfully mistreated, she was in a terrible state. Avery and the International League for the Protection of Horses had rescued her. Issie couldn't believe it when Avery told her he wanted Issie to be her guardian and take care of the mare.

It was a lot for him to ask. Until Blaze turned up, Issie had sworn off horses for good. She didn't want anything more to do with them after what had happened to Mystic.

Mystic had been Issie's first ever horse. A fourteen-hand, swaybacked grey gelding with faded dapples and a shaggy mane. Issie had loved Mystic deeply from the first day they met. When Mystic had been killed in a road accident at the pony club, Issie thought she would never get over it. She was sure she would never have another horse. But Avery knew better. He brought Blaze to her and together the broken-hearted girl and the broken-spirited pony healed each other and became a real team.

And Mystic? His death was just the beginning of a whole new adventure. Issie's bond with Mystic was more powerful than even she suspected. In fact Mystic wasn't truly gone at all. Whenever things got really bad, whenever Issie needed him most, he would be there at her side – not like a ghost or anything like that, but a real horse, flesh and blood.

Mystic was her guardian angel. He had saved her and Blaze countless times now. She hadn't seen the grey gelding in a long time, but she felt his presence more strongly than ever now that Blaze was close to foaling. Just knowing that the grey gelding was watching over Blaze and protecting her made Issie feel better about leaving the mare behind.

"I have to go, but Mystic will keep an eye on you, OK, girl?" Issie murmured as the mare nuzzled against her. Then she gave Blaze one more carrot for the road and left the mare in the paddock, heading home to pack her bags.

But when she got home, Issie was surprised to find her bags already packed and her sleeping bag rolled and ready at the front door.

"Mum?" Issie called out. Mrs Brown emerged from the kitchen.

"There you are!" she said breezily. "I figured you'd be running late so I went ahead and packed for you. I've washed and folded all that stuff you had in your laundry basket and put that in, and you've got three pairs of jodhpurs, your new hoodie and your *PONY Magazines…*"

"But Mum, I thought you didn't really want me to go," Issie said.

"Well, I was hoping you'd get a nice, safe, ordinary part-time job on the supermarket check-out for the holidays." Mrs Brown put her arms round Issie and gave her a hug. "But then I realised you wouldn't be my Issie if you did that, would you?"

Mrs Brown's hug got tighter. "I've told Hester to take good care of you this time, and I'll be there to pick you up and bring you home at the weekend." She let go of Issie and smiled. "Your dinner is ready – go and sit at the table. After that, you better get straight up to bed. You have an early start in the morning."

Issie did go straight to bed after dinner and she was so exhausted she had no trouble falling asleep. The last thing she remembered was setting her alarm clock for six. Then she was dreaming. In her dream she could hear Avery calling to her. He was telling her to hurry up because Blaze was having the foal. Issie could hear the foaling monitor going *parp! parp! parp!* telling her that she must go to her mare, but it was like her limbs were made of lead, it was so hard to move. Then, as she drowsily woke up out of her sleep, she realised the noise wasn't a foaling alarm at all. It was the sound of her alarm clock and there was her mother, sitting beside her on the bed and shaking her gently by the shoulder.

"Issie! It's time to get going. I came in and woke you up already, but you must have gone straight back to sleep," Mrs Brown said. "Come on. Everyone is here waiting for you."

"What time is it now?" Issie mumbled, rubbing her eyes.

"Seven o'clock."

"Ohmygod!"

Issie leapt out of bed. She pulled on her dressing gown and ran to the window on the other side of the hallway, the one that looked out to the main street. Aidan's horse truck was already parked outside. Issie could see Stella, Kate and Natasha waving madly through the truck windows at her. Stella was mouthing something at her but Issie couldn't hear her. "What?" she called back. Stella looked exasperated and wound down her window. "I said hurry up, sleepyhead!" she laughed. "We've been waiting for ages!"

"Yeah, come on!" Kate grinned at her.

Natasha glared at her balefully. "Typical," she said. "Making the rest of us wait for you."

"Sorry! I'm coming. Give me five minutes!" Issie called back.

There was barely time for a shower and no time for breakfast. Mrs Brown managed to thrust a piece of Marmite toast in Issie's hand and give her daughter a kiss goodbye as she raced out of the door.

Outside the horse truck was waiting. A boy stood by the door of the truck cab. He was wearing black jeans and a flannel shirt and his long dark hair fell in a floppy fringe over his face. "I've put your bags in the truck. The others are all sitting in the back, but I thought you might like to ride up in the cab with me," Aidan said.

Aidan! Issie could feel her heart beating fast in her chest and her mouth was so dry there was no way she could choke down the last bite of the Marmite toast. "Uh-huh," she managed.

Aidan looked pleased and gave her a shy smile, pushing his fringe back so that Issie could see his startling blue eyes. "Let's go then!"

The first five minutes of the drive were excruciatingly painful. Issie didn't know what to say so the pair of them sat there in silence looking out the window.

Finally Aidan spoke. "Do you know much about this movie?"

"I've read the book, like, a hundred times," Issie said. "There's this princess – her name is Galatea, but everyone calls her Gala. She's the ruler of a kingdom where the women are all princesses and brave warriors – but she's the strongest of them all and she has superpowers and stuff. Anyway, in Galatea's realm the horses are all palominos and they have magical powers too. Then there are all these really creepy guys called the Elerians. The Elerians have these black horses, and the really horrible part is that their horses were all once palominos too. They used to belong to Galatea's stables, but one by one the Elerians have captured them and turned them into the Horses of Darkness. The Elerians are actually vampires – except they bite horses, not people. They use their vampire fangs to suck all the life out of the palominos and turn them into these awful black horses, drained of all their pure strength and overcome by evil…"

Issie suddenly turned to look at Aidan. Why was he smiling at her? "What?" she said defensively. "What's so funny?"

"Nothing's funny!" Aidan said, still smiling. "It's just that I'd forgotten how excited you get about stuff – especially horses. I really like that about you."

Issie fumbled around in her bag. "Here," she said, handing Aidan a dog-eared paperback. "I brought my copy with me. You can borrow it if you like."

Aidan smiled. "I've already read it. It's one of my favourite books too."

After that, Issie and Aidan talked non-stop and the hour-long drive seemed to take no time at all. The horse truck thundered along the road past the pine forests north of Chevalier Point, through rolling green fields dotted with grazing cows. Finally they pulled off the main road down a gravel driveway and Issie was surprised when they were stopped by a burly security guard at the farm gate.

"There have been loads of paparazzi – tabloid newspaper photographers – trying to get on the set," Aidan explained to Issie as they drove on again through the paddocks. "Apparently the girl they've got playing Princess Galatea is really famous. There's been loads of rumours. They're trying to keep everything hush-hush. Even the crew haven't been told who it is…"

But Issie wasn't really listening to him. She was too busy looking out the front window of the truck.

"Ohmygod!" she breathed. "Aidan! This is incredible!"

As they came over the hill, there in front of them was a grand golden gate that led to a vast white cobbled courtyard and in the centre was a gold fountain, with life-size statues of rearing horses spouting brilliant turquoise water from their golden mouths. Surrounding the white courtyard were rows of white loose boxes with golden doors.

"The stables of Princess Galatea," Aidan grinned. He turned the horse truck past the golden gates. "And over there is the black castle of Eleria."

Issie looked to her left and saw the familiar sight of Chevalier Castle. Only the castle didn't look like it usually did. The ruins, which sat on top of a hill that looked out over farmland and forest, had been sprayed with black paint. The broad, cobblestone terraces that wound round and round like a corkscrew to the summit had also been painted black. The castle, with spikes on its turrets and a huge iron portcullis, would have been a terrifying vision if it weren't for the crew members and builders running about the place. Everywhere you looked there were set dressers lugging enormous black-varnished styrofoam boulders towards the castle or painting fake green slime on the drawbridge.

"Production has been under way for weeks now. These are just the finishing touches. They're nearly ready to start filming," Aidan said.

He turned the truck around and parked it near the golden gates of the stables, giving a cheery wave to one of the set dressers who was busily pouring more turquoise dye into the golden fountain.

"We brought all the horses here a month ago – Hester has done loads of desensitising work with them. They've filmed some of the vampire riders' scenes already – but the main stunts need palomino riders too and that's where you come in." He jumped out of the truck cab, followed by Issie.

"I'll give you a proper tour later, but first let's get

you all settled in. Your rooms are over there behind the stable block. We'll grab your bags. It's easier if we walk through from here."

As Aidan said this, the door swung open on the side of the truck and Stella, Kate and Natasha emerged.

"Whoa!" Stella said, looking at the golden stables. "Is this where we'll be staying?"

The others laughed.

"The golden stables!" Kate squealed. "They're just like I always imagined they'd look!"

"I know," Issie beamed. "Isn't it cool?"

Natasha was the last to climb out of the truck. She cast a disdainful glance at Aidan.

"Well? Where are our rooms?" she demanded, gesturing at the luggage lying on the ground. "Come on! Bring my bags, will you?"

Stella rounded on Natasha immediately. "Aidan's not your servant, you know. We all carry our own bags around here."

"Oh, really?" Natasha glared at her. "Mummy always told me that ladies never carry luggage. I'm not sure what your mother taught you…"

Before Stella could snap back, they were interrupted by the sight of the most enormous car they'd ever seen cruising towards them down the driveway.

"What is that?" Kate said as the chrome-yellow Hummer with black tinted windows pulled up next to them.

"You mean *who* is that, don't you?" Aidan said. "I have a feeling we're finally going to discover who's got the starring role in *The Palomino Princess*."

As the rest of the crew ran over to the Hummer and gathered round, the front doors of the vehicle swung open and two men in black suits wearing earpiece microphones jumped out.

"Who are they? I don't recognise them. Are they famous?" Issie whispered to Aidan.

"I think they're just the bodyguards," Aidan whispered back.

The bodyguards spoke into their earpieces and nodded to each other. Then one of the men stood guard while the other opened the back door of the Hummer. From behind the tinted glass a girl emerged, helped down by a third bodyguard.

"Ohmygod! I don't believe it! It's the Teen Drama Queen!" Stella squealed.

"Stella!" Issie hissed at her. "Don't! You'll embarrass her!"

The girl, who had clearly heard Stella's comment,

pushed her dark glasses back to reveal her violet eyes. "Don't worry," she said in a soft mid-west American accent. "People always call me that. I get it, like, all the time." She smiled, revealing her perfect white teeth. "Are y'all working on the movie?" she asked.

"Ummm, yes. We're stunt riders," Issie said. "My name is Isadora and this is Stella and Kate, Natasha and Aidan."

"Nice to meet y'all." The girl smiled again. "I'm Angelique Adams."

Chapter 3

Issie couldn't believe it. Angelique Adams! The girl that *Sixteen Magazine* called "the most famous teenager in the world" was standing right in front of her.

Angelique looked just like she did on all those magazine covers. Her long honey-blonde hair was ironed straight and she had a deep golden tan. Dressed in designer jeans, a leather vest and enormous sunglasses, she looked much smaller than she did in her movies. Issie was actually ever so slightly taller than the pint-sized celebrity.

Angelique clicked her fingers and two more people leapt out of the back of the Hummer – a dark-haired woman and a blond man.

"Her entourage," whispered Aidan under his breath

to Issie. Angelique gestured to the woman who scurried forward and handed her a coffee. Angelique took a quick sip and then thrust the cup back at her assistant as the blond man darted in and began to fuss around, fixing her hair, pulling make-up brushes out of his belt to add some blusher and a fresh coat of lip gloss.

"That's enough, Tony!" Angelique snapped, pushing the make-up man out of the way just in time as the gang of paparazzi photographers, who had been tailing the Hummer, all leapt out of their cars. They jostled each other to get close to Angelique and began to take her picture, their motor drives whirring, cameras flashing.

"Angelique!" the paparazzi shouted to her. "Over here! Look this way. Give us a smile, Angelique!"

Suddenly there was a noise at the back of the paparazzi pack. "Lemme through!" A little man in a khaki army jacket was leaping up and down like Rumpelstiltskin, elbowing his way past the photographers. "One side, comin' through!" he snapped as he barged his way forward. When the little man reached the front and found himself blocked by Angelique's bodyguards he began to shout even louder. "Hey! You big apes! Yes, you! Lemme through I tell ya!"

The little man was lugging an enormous video camera on his shoulder. He was accompanied by a pale thin man carrying what looked a bit like a fluffy grey cat pinned to the end of a long stick.

"I'm with Angelique!" the man insisted to the bodyguards. "I have an access-all-areas pass. She'll tell you, won't you, Angelique, baby? Tell them!" he pleaded.

Angelique looked over and gave a nod to the bodyguards to let the man and his skinny sidekick through. The other paparazzi began to complain loudly at this and the little man gave them a smirk. "A-list access!" he beamed. Then he turned to the teen starlet and smiled his oiliest grin.

"Angelique! Honey!" His voice took on a crawly tone. "Great entrance, baby! Right on! But... uhhh, the thing is, we've had a slight technical hitch and we're going to have to reshoot all of that."

Angelique's smile disappeared. The little man looked nervous. "It's all because of Bob here," he stammered. "He didn't get the sound recorded right. Isn't that right, Bob?" He shot a withering glare at his sidekick, who looked suitably guilty and didn't say anything.

"So... we need you to do it again from the top," the little man said. "Can you get back in the car and then drive up and do the whole arriving-on-set thing again? And make it really, you know, *real*."

Angelique rolled her eyes. "All right. But this better not take all day, Eugene!" she snapped at him. "I've got, like, a masseuse and three beauticians waiting for me back at my trailer."

She glared at Bob, who cowered a little, then she clicked her fingers at her assistants and climbed back into the Hummer. Her bodyguards quickly piled in after them, slamming the car into reverse as the paparazzi scrambled to get out of their way.

"Hey, you kids!" the man in the khaki jacket turned his attention to Issie and her friends.

"Who us?" Stella said.

"What? Yes, you! Of course you!" the man said. "You kids were great!" he enthused. "We'll go once more, just like last time. Are you ready?"

Stella looked at him blankly. "Ready for what?"

"The second take of course!" the little man said. There were more blank looks from Stella and Issie. The man sighed. He didn't have time for this.

"We're making a documentary here, kids! The name is Eugene – Eugene Sneadly – Hollywood's most hardworking documentary film-maker." Eugene gestured over his shoulder at the skinny man with the cat on a stick. "This here is Bob, my sound man. That stick of his is what we call a sound boom. Hey, watch it with that thing, Bob!"

Eugene cast a surly look at Bob and then continued, "Bob and I are here with Angelique Adams. She's given us A-list priority on the film set so that we can do this behind-the-scenes documentary about her. *Drama Queen – Behind the Scenes.* That's what we're calling it. Sounds exciting, right? And it is! It's gonna be big, big, big, baby, because everyone loves Angelique and, well, the girl just can't help herself. Like they say, she's a regular, real-life drama queen."

"You just got lucky, kids," Eugene went on, barely pausing for breath. "This is gonna be your big moment. You can all be in my documentary. So get ready to go wild because… Angelique Adams is about to arrive!"

"But she's already arrived," Stella protested. "We just met her."

The little man sighed. Then he raised his hands to the sky and began talking to himself. "Oh, Eugene, Eugene! Why are you working with amateurs here?" He looked back at Stella.

"I know she's already arrived, sweetheart," he said through gritted teeth. "What I'm saying is, let's pretend and do it again, shall we?"

The girls and Aidan all nodded at this. They weren't sure what Eugene was up to, but it seemed easiest to agree and go along with it.

"And… action!" Eugene shouted, waving his hand frantically at the Hummer in the distance.

The chrome-yellow car drove down the road and pulled up in front of the stables for a seond time. The doors opened and Angelique appeared, looking every bit as fresh-faced and eager to meet everyone as she had the first time round.

"Hi!" she smiled sweetly. "Nice to meet y'all. I'm Angelique Adams!"

The girls and Aidan were dumbstruck as the paparazzi bounded after her and started snapping wildly once more and Angelique grinned and waved.

"Perfect! Perfect!" Eugene yelled out. "Got it! Great work, Angelique."

As soon as the cameras stopped rolling Angelique abruptly stopped smiling. "That's it, Eugene! I'm outta here."

"But, baby, Rupert ain't even here yet. He wants to meet you. They start shooting tomorrow," Eugene said.

"Y'all can wait for him if you want, Eugene. I'll be in my trailer gettin' a spray tan!" Angelique snapped. She hopped back in the Hummer, obediently followed by her assistants and bodyguards who slammed the door and promptly floored it.

"Angelique, cupcake! Wait! We're coming too!" Eugene cried. He and the paparazzi made a dash for their cars. Clouds of dust and gravel flew up from the road as the Hummer sped off with a line of cars following closely behind.

"I thought the security guard at the gate was supposed to keep the photographers out," Issie said to Aidan.

Aidan shrugged. "I guess Angelique let them in. Maybe she likes the paparazzi following her everywhere. You know, taking her picture for all those magazines."

"I still don't believe we just met Angelique Adams!" Stella said. "She is soooo famous!"

Natasha sighed. "Yeah, she seemed real thrilled to meet you too, Stella. She couldn't wait to get away! Didn't you notice how fast she got out of here?"

Natasha glanced around. "Not that I blame her for wanting to get away from this place," she muttered under her breath, just loud enough for everyone to hear.

Aidan ignored Natasha and picked up her bags. It was clear that he was going to have to carry her luggage since the snooty blonde still refused to do it herself.

"Grab your bags," he instructed the others. "I'll show you to the barracks."

"What do you mean 'barracks'?" Natasha said as she followed along behind him through the white courtyard of the stables. "Surely we all have our own private trailers? Aidan? Aidan!"

They walked straight through the golden stables and on the other side they found themselves standing in front of a row of makeshift wooden huts.

"These really were army barracks once," Aidan explained. "Rupert, the director, bought them cheap and had them moved on to the site to use as accommodation for the crew."

Aidan pointed to the left. "That building over there is where the props department and the set builders live. And over there are the sleeping quarters for the Elerian horsemen – that's where I'm staying." He pointed to the right. "Those two silver trailers are the costume department and make-up and that white building next to the trailers is the main dining hall where we all meet for meals."

"This is your barrack." Aidan gestured to the building directly in front of them. "Palomino wranglers' quarters!" he grinned. "Come on inside."

The wooden barracks turned out to be much

plusher inside than they looked. The lounge was really cosy with lots of colourful beanbags, plump sofas and a wide-screen TV. Beyond the main lounge was a hallway with three doors leading off. Each doorway opened on to a bunk room.

"The room at the end is Hester's," Aidan explained. "That leaves two rooms for you guys to share."

Stella stuck her head round the corner of the first bunk room. It had three single beds. "I bagsy this bed!" she cried, flinging herself on the best bunk underneath the window.

"I'll go here then!" Kate said, heaving her bags up on to the bed closest to the door.

That left one more bunk in the room. Issie looked at it. Then she looked over at Natasha. The snooty blonde was milling about out in the hallway, pretending she wasn't even slightly interested in the sleeping arrangements.

If Issie took the third bunk, she realised, she would be sharing a room with Stella and Kate, which was great. But that also meant Natasha would be left out, all by herself in the other room. Issie picked up her bag. "Hey, Natasha?" she said. "Do you want to come with me and check out our room?"

Natasha looked at Issie with grateful eyes. "OK," she said cheerfully. She grabbed her bags and began to walk ahead of Issie down the hall. Then she turned back and added, "But don't get any ideas because I'm having the bunk by the window."

As Issie unpacked her bags and filled the chest of drawers next to her bunk, Natasha opened the windows for some fresh air and fussed about the state of the bed linen, which was "cheap cotton, not proper Egyptian like at home" and the bunks, which were "like concrete and totally impossible to sleep on".

"You didn't have to come, you know!" Issie snapped, but as soon as she said it, she wished she hadn't.

Natasha stopped unpacking. She glared at Issie. "Why did you ask me then?"

"What do you mean?"

"Why did you ask me to come? Was it just because you needed another rider?" Natasha sneered. "You must have been desperate. I know you and Stella and Kate don't actually like me, so it's not like you asked me because I'm your friend or anything…"

"Natasha, no, it wasn't like that…" Issie began, but Natasha cut her off.

"I know what you all think of me, you know. I'm not

stupid. You think I'm stuck up just because I go to a private school."

"Well…" Issie began, uncertain what to say to this.

"I know you say horrible things about me," Natasha insisted. "Well, not you so much. You aren't so bad, I suppose, Issie. But Stella is always being mean to me."

"But, Natasha!" Issie protested, "you always say mean things to her too! You kind of bring it on yourself, you know."

Natasha shrugged at this. "Anyway, you don't have to share a room with me. I don't care. Go ahead if you'd rather be with your friends."

Issie shook her head. "No. It's OK, honest. I don't want to move," she said. "I like this room. I think it'll be fun to share together."

This seemed to cheer Natasha up a bit and she began to unpack her clothes, laying them carefully into the drawers.

"I'm glad your mum let you come," Issie said.

"Oh, Mummy was desperate for me to come!" Natasha said. "She couldn't wait to get rid of me."

"What do you mean?" Issie was confused.

"You mean you don't know?" Natasha looked shocked. "I thought everyone had heard about it." She began to pull random things out of her bag, throwing her T-shirts violently into the drawer. "My parents have split up. They're getting a divorce. They're so busy arguing with each other, they barely notice that I'm in the room." Natasha's face was flushed with embarrassment. "I thought that was why you asked me to come. I thought your mum made you ask me because of the divorce."

"No," Issie said. "No, I didn't know. Mum didn't make me ask you – I just thought, well, I thought we might have fun."

Natasha seemed to perk up a little at this. "You know," she said as she arranged her hairbrush and lip gloss on the dressing table, "it will be fun! It'll be like a sleepover." She was smiling. "I've got loads of treats like chocolate fudge in my bag for us to share. We can eat lollies and tell ghost stories and… ohmygod! Argghh!"

Natasha leapt up on to her bunk squealing with fear as three enormous dogs suddenly bowled into the room; their claws scratched against the wooden floorboards as they ran about panting, sniffing and slobbering.

"Ewww! Get them away from me!" Natasha howled.

"Strudel! Taxi! Nanook! Lie down!" Issie ordered. The dogs obeyed immediately and dropped down on the floor, lying perfectly still with their heads on their paws.

"Aunty Hess?" Issie called out. "Is that you? I'm in here!" Through the doorway behind the dogs came a glamorous woman with shoulder-length, curly blonde hair, dressed in black jodhpurs and a crisp white blouse.

"Isadora! My favourite niece!" Hester beamed as she grabbed Issie in an enormous hug. Issie found herself squished in her aunt's arms, drowning in the familiar scent of Chanel perfume.

"Aunty Hess! It's so good to see you again!" Issie said. She turned to Natasha. "Aunty Hess, I want you to meet my friend Natasha from pony club. She's a really good rider."

"Hello, Natasha. How terrific to have you here!" Hester smiled.

Natasha smiled back stiffly. "Thank you," she replied.

"And these are Hester's dogs," Issie said, finishing her introductions. "This is Nanook," she explained, pointing to the shaggy black Newfoundland, "and Strudel," she said, patting the golden retriever. "And this one is Taxi," Issie said, scratching the black and white cattle dog behind the ears.

Natasha looked nervously at the dogs and still didn't get down off the bunk.

"Good boys! Outside now!" Hester instructed the

dogs – and the three of them leapt up immediately, tearing off out the door.

"Are you girls unpacking? There's time for that later. Right now you're coming with me," Hester said firmly. "Go and get the others. It's time to meet the horses."

Chapter 4

Issie had been wondering about the horses. She hadn't seen any sign of them at the golden stables. "No, no," Hester laughed. "The golden stables are just a movie set. We don't actually keep the horses there!" She pointed down the road which ran in the opposite direction behind the barracks. "The stables are down the hill. Much less grand than the film set version, I'm afraid."

Hester was right. The real stables weren't trimmed with gold or anything flashy. Still, Issie thought they were totally amazing. The stable block was enormous, with a huge indoor arena in the middle of it where the riders could train. Two long rows of loose boxes ran down either side, where the horses were stabled.

"We arrived here and began training and preparing

the horses for filming last month," Hester explained as she beckoned them to follow her through the arena towards the stables. "We've already shot a few scenes with the vampire riders. Now, over the next two weeks, while you girls are here, we'll do the rest of the big stunt work."

"Two weeks!" Stella squeaked. "That's not much time, is it?"

"Most of the movie will be finished off back at the studio – they do all the special effects on blue screen," Hester said. "You girls are here to film the stunt double work. You'll all double for the princess riders. You'll be riding the scenes instead of the real actors; sometimes you'll even get to speak their lines. Then they'll use special effects back at the studio to replace your faces with the movie stars' and make it look like they were the ones riding the horses the whole time."

"But won't it look fake?" Stella asked.

"This is the movies, dear. Nothing is really real," Hester grinned. "Come on, I'll introduce you to the real stars of *The Palomino Princess*." She led them to a row of loose boxes.

"There are thirteen horses in total living here," Hester said. "Eight black horses and five palominos."

"But why do you need so many black horses?" Kate

asked. "In the book there are only seven vampire riders."

"We're using two different horses to play the role of Dante – the black horse ridden by Francis the vampire king," Hester said. "One horse will be Dante for all the action sequences and chase scenes. The other horse will do the close-up work. We'll make it look like the same horse of course, but it won't be."

She unbolted the top half of the Dutch door of the stall, swinging it back on its hinges, and a black and white piebald face came out to greet them.

"Diablo!" Issie cried, delighted to see the black and white Quarter Horse once more.

Kate looked confused. "But you said you were only using black horses! How come Diablo is here?"

"We'll put black dye on his white patches," Hester smiled. She ran her hand down Diablo's nose. "You'll never be able to tell that he's dyed when you see him at a distance." She stroked the big piebald on his soft muzzle. "Diablo will play Dante in the chase sequences, like the scene in the forest when Francis is after Galatea."

Hester opened the next stall. "Diablo is a good stunt horse, but he's not pretty enough for the close-ups. For those we need a really dramatic, handsome horse with a long mane," she said, "and that's what Destiny is here for."

Issie hardly recognised Destiny in his loose box. The stallion had changed so much since she saw him last. When she first met Destiny he had been running wild with the Blackthorn Ponies. She remembered his sun-bleached black coat, caked in mud and his mane and tail, ratty and tangled from his wild life. Aunt Hester had spent the past few months putting in long hours grooming the stallion and now he was completely changed. He gleamed like a show horse. His coat was like black satin and his mane and tail were long, glossy and jet-black. Issie noticed that even the white stripe on his elegant Swedish Warmblood face had been dyed so that he was totally black all over.

"Hey, boy, remember me?" Issie called to him over the stable door. Destiny pricked up his ears at Issie's voice and came over to her. He nickered softly as Issie stroked his nose, then rubbed his head against her jacket until she produced a carrot for him.

"Well!" Hester said. "Look at that! He won't give the stable hands the time of day. He's not even this affectionate with me or Aidan. He obviously remembers you, Isadora."

"You're such a beauty, aren't you, Destiny?" Issie said, running her hands down the stallion's glossy neck.

"He is looking marvellous, isn't he?" Hester beamed with pride. "I've been training him with Aidan, who's stunt-doubling for the actor who plays Francis. Aidan handles Destiny nicely. It's not easy with a stallion – as well you know, Isadora – after all, you were the one who broke him in."

Natasha let out an incredulous snort at this. "Yeah, right... sure she did!"

"She did, Natasha!" Stella leapt to Issie's defence. "We were all there. We saw it. Issie broke Destiny in all by herself – well, with a bit of help from Tom. And she did it in one day too!"

Natasha could see that she was outnumbered. "What-ever," she said, rolling her eyes at Stella. Then she turned to Aunt Hester. "I'm bored now. Is this tour going to take all day?"

Aunt Hester gave Natasha a steely look. "I expect you're keen to get down to work, are you, Natasha? These stables could really do with mucking out. You'll find your roster on the inside of the main stable door."

"What do you mean 'mucking out'?" Natasha said.

"Well, dear, surely you didn't think the horses would look after themselves?" Hester said. "It's part of the palomino wrangler's job to look after all the horses, doing the feeding and grooming and mucking out. As I said, the roster is on the door. In fact," Hester said to Natasha, "I believe you're rostered on for dung duty first. Would you like to get started now or would you like to come with the rest of us and meet the palominos?"

Natasha's face furrowed into a scowl, but she didn't say anything as Hester led them across the arena to another row of stalls.

"This is where my girls are stabled," Hester said. She moved along the row of stalls, opening the top of the first four Dutch doors. One by one, the golden palominos thrust their heads over the partitions of their loose boxes.

"Hey! I know those two," Stella said, pointing to the horses in the second and third stalls. "It's Paris and Nicole!"

"Well spotted!" Hester smiled. "My own two palominos from Blackthorn Farm. I am impressed that you could tell them apart from the others." She pointed to the palominos in stalls one and four. "These ones are my new girls, Rosie and Athena." Rosie and Athena were just as pretty as Paris and Nicole with white blazes down their palomino noses and dark sooty muzzles.

"Rosie is a great stunt pony. She's green but she learns fast. You'll be riding her, Natasha," Hester said. "Athena is my reserve – a back-up in case one of the other mares goes lame or something goes wrong. I don't want any problems with the horses to hold up the filming. Rupert, the director, is on a tight schedule."

"You mean just swap one horse for another?" Stella asked.

"Why not, dear? After all, they all look so alike, don't they?" Hester smiled. "Except for Stardust. She's got that X-factor that makes her special. You'll see what I mean. Come with me and I'll introduce you to my new superstar!" Hester moved down the stable aisle now to the last stall in the row and unbolted the door.

"Girls," she said grandly, "I'd like you to meet Galatica Supernova – or Stardust as she's known on the set."

As if on cue, Stardust poked her head over the stall. Hester was right – the mare was a true beauty. She was larger than the other palominos, nearly fifteen-two, and her coat was darker and glossier, the colour of warm treacle. Her mane was so white it was almost silver. "She looks like a Barbie doll!" Issie laughed. "She's so pretty and perfect it's almost like she's not real."

"She's real – and she's a real handful too!" Hester said. "Stardust is supposed to play Seraphine, Princess Galatea's horse." Hester shook her head. "It's the most important role in the film. But our training sessions haven't been going very well so far. Have they, Stardust?"

As she spoke, Hester reached out to give Stardust a friendly pat, but Stardust shook her head indignantly. Then, completely without warning, the mare lunged over the stable door. Her teeth were bared as she tried to land a nip on Aunt Hester's arm.

Hester was too fast for her. She had been working around horses for far too many years to be caught out so easily. Instead, she sidestepped quickly, avoiding Stardust's teeth, then turned round and grabbed the mare with a tight hold on her halter before she could try it again.

Stardust's ears were flat back against her head in anger as she fought to free herself from Hester's hands. The palomino's eyes had turned dark with fury.

"You see?" Hester sighed. "She's a naughty little madam. I'm at my wits' end trying to deal with her."

"Why don't you just use one of the other palominos instead," Natasha sniffed.

"It's not that simple," Hester said. "Stardust might be troublesome, but she's also very talented. She can rear on command, she can nod and shake her head on cue and she can perform all sorts of tricks that none of my other palominos have mastered. Plus she's gorgeous.

Rupert says that the camera loves her. He's the director and he's the one who cast Stardust to be his Seraphine."

"But why did he choose her if she's so badly behaved?" Kate asked.

Hester sighed. "That's the thing! Stardust wasn't always like this. She used to be one of the best horses in the movie business. When her owners offered to let me use her for this film, I jumped at the chance to cast her. I didn't realise what a drama I was in for."

Issie looked at the palomino. Stardust had her ears flat back still, as if she was waiting for her chance to strike again. Hester sighed and let go of the halter, and the mare threw her head up and reared back, immediately heading back into the stall, standing at a distance where no one could reach her. She stood there, pawing restlessly at the floor of the loose box, shaking her head as if to say, "Go away and leave me alone!"

"Her owners finally admitted to me that they knew she was having problems," Hester said. "They say it all went wrong on her last film. Bad handlers apparently. I suspect they didn't know what they were doing and so when Stardust wouldn't perform for them, they got quite rough with her."

"Poor Stardust," Stella said. She clucked over the stall

door at the palomino mare, but Stardust just glowered back at her from the corner, her ears still flat against her head. Stella looked at the expression on the mare's face and stepped away from the stable door.

"Her owners said they were hoping that working on this film with me would turn Stardust back into her old self again." Hester shook her head. "But I'm not so sure. She's a very sensitive mare. I've tried to put the extra time in with her, but she isn't responding. She's developed some frightful vices – she bites and kicks, she's unpredictable to ride."

Hester sighed. "I have thirteen horses here and I've had my hands full with the vampire riders. I simply don't have time for prima-donna palominos." She turned to Issie. "So I thought maybe you'd like to take over."

"What?" Issie squeaked.

"Issie, I'm at the end of my tether," Hester said, looking serious. "We're about to start filming Seraphine's scenes and we're no closer to sorting Stardust out than we were a whole month ago when she arrived on set." Hester shook her head. "At this rate Stardust is going to hold up filming. If filming is delayed because of my horses, it could cost millions. I haven't had the nerve to tell Rupert that we're having trouble with her. He's got enough on his plate keeping the actors in line without worrying about problem palominos. Seraphine, I mean Stardust, needs to be the perfect angel in front of those cameras when we start filming next week or Rupert will blow his top." Hester paused. "Isadora, I want you and Aidan to work with her. I'll take care of the other horses if you two knuckle down and focus on her training. You must get Stardust to behave like her old self again. I need my palomino princess back on form in time for filming to begin next week."

"Me?" Issie was stunned. "Well, I can try, I suppose…"

"You'll have to do better than that, Isadora," Hester said darkly. "This is Stardust's last chance."

Chapter 5

The mood was very gloomy at the palomino barracks the next morning.

"What do you think Hester meant?" Stella asked. "You know, when she said this was Stardust's last chance?"

"I heard her mutter something about 'glue factory'," said Natasha, who was lying on the sofa in front of the big-screen TV trying to get the remote to work.

"You didn't!" Stella snapped. "You're just making that up!"

Natasha glared at her. "That's what I heard," she said. "I don't care if you believe me or not."

"Well, she's not going to the glue factory anyway," Kate huffed. "Poor Stardust. She's been mistreated, that's all. She's not really bad natured."

"She looked pretty bad when she was trying to sink her teeth into Hester's arm if you ask me!" Natasha said.

"No one did ask you though, did they?" Stella said. "In fact, I can't figure out why anyone even asked you to come on this trip in the first place."

"Hey! Don't take it out on me, Stella!" Natasha shrugged. "It's not my fault that palomino is going to be petfood. There's no point in… Hey! This TV has cable!" Now that Natasha had figured out the remote control, she gave up on fighting with Stella as she channel-surfed. She flicked through until she struck the E! channel.

"Hey look, Stella!" Natasha smirked. "*The E! True Hollywood Story.* It's all about your NBF, Angelique Adams." Angelique was talking to an E! reporter about her new role in the upcoming movie, *The Palomino Princess.*

"It's a dream come true working on this film," Angelique gushed. "Rupert Conrad is the hottest director in Hollywood right now. I was desperate to work with him. It's so funny because when I heard Rupert wanted a real rider for the part of Galatea I was, like, that's totally me! I've been riding all my life since I was, like, a baby, and when this role came up everyone said it was perfect for me because I am such a great rider. I am, like, totally the Palomino Princess!"

Angelique gave the reporter a flash of her big white smile.

The reporter smiled back. "This film has a lot of great horse action in it, Angelique," he said, "but we hear that most of it will actually be done with stunt riders and special effects. Will you be using a stunt double?"

"No way, y'all!" Angelique smiled at him and flicked her long blonde hair. "Rupert says he wants me to really get into the role of Princess Galatea. I'm going to be doing all my own stunts."

"Wow! I didn't know she was a really good rider too!" Kate said, looking impressed.

Issie shrugged. "Me neither. That's pretty cool."

"Maybe she'll be able to handle Stardust then?" Stella said hopefully.

"If she's riding her own stunts, she should come down and join our training session," Issie said. "Aunty Hess wants us all at the arena first thing tomorrow to put the palominos through the desensitisation course."

"I wish we didn't have costume fittings today," Stella grumbled. "I really want to start riding."

"Ohmygod! The costume fitting!" Kate looked at her watch. "We're due there right now!"

"Are you coming, Natasha?" Issie asked. "They said we all had to be there."

Natasha groaned and reluctantly turned off the TV, dragging herself up off the sofa and following the other girls out of the barracks to the costume trailer.

The silver trailer was like a caravan only much longer and it had the words COSTUME DEPARTMENT written across the door in bright purple letters.

The girls had just reached the door and Stella had her hand out to grab the handle when it suddenly swung open. Standing in front of them was a woman in a brown hippy skirt and peasant blouse; she had curly hair down to her waist.

"Hi, I'm Amber," the woman said. "I'm Head of Costume. You guys are the stunt riders, right?" She smiled at them. "Come in! We're just finishing up. You're next."

Issie stepped up the silver stairs into the trailer. Inside it was like a gypsy tea room. The walls were draped with floral scarves and covered with mirrors trimmed with glowing lightbulbs. There were tea chests overflowing with clothes and prop boxes stuffed with swords and lances.

In the middle of the room stood a tall man, dressed in a black monk's robe with an enormous hood. As the girls all piled into the trailer, the man turned to face them, flicking back the hood to reveal his bulbous bald head which was covered with ugly purple veins.

"Hi!" The man smiled pleasantly at them. His voice sounded familiar somehow, Issie thought. "Did Hester introduce you to the horses? Isn't Stardust a stunner? Bit naughty though…"

"Aidan?" Issie was shocked. "Ohmygod! Aidan? Is that really you?"

Aidan nodded. "It's amazing what a latex bald wig and two hours in the make-up chair will do for my good looks."

Stella giggled at this and elbowed Issie. "You didn't recognise your own boyfriend!"

Issie blushed furiously, hoping that Aidan hadn't heard what Stella had just said.

"Hey, check this out!" Aidan said to the girls. He reached into the pocket of his black robe then hid his face for a moment beneath the hood of his cloak. Then he flipped the hood back and smiled again, revealing a pair of long white vampire fangs.

"Ohmygod!" Stella shrieked.

"Scary, huh?" Aidan said. "They look great but it's hard to ride in them. I keep biting my tongue."

"Hey, guess who else is riding?" Stella said. "We just found out that Angelique Adams is going to be doing all her own stunts. It turns out she's totally horse-mad!"

"Really?" Aidan raised an eyebrow at this news. "I didn't pick Angelique for a horsy girl. If she's riding, why haven't I even seen her on the set yet?"

"Maybe she's so good she doesn't need to practise," Stella said.

"All right then." Aidan flicked his black hood back up and bared his fangs. "I'd better get going. We've got dress rehearsals for the vampire horsemen… but first I might have a bite to eat…" He made a sudden lunge at Issie as if he were about to sink his fangs into her. Issie shrieked and leapt back and the other girls and Aidan began laughing.

"I'm not a real vampire, you know," Aidan grinned at her as he ducked out the trailer door. "I promise I won't bite."

As Aidan bounded out of the trailer, Amber the costume lady came back in with an armful of clothes. She put the clothes down on a chair in the corner and then looked Issie up and down. "You're a size ten, right? Here – take this blouse and these jodhpurs. You can go into that changing room over there to put them on."

Amber gestured to a row of four changing cubicles built into the wall of the trailer. She passed Issie a pile of silver, blue and white clothes and then turned her attention to Stella, Kate and Natasha.

"I'll get you all dressed and sorted and then you can go next door and do make-up try-outs after that," she said.

Issie walked into the changing room and held up her costume. There was a pair of sky-blue jodhpurs that looked about her size, and a flowing white blouse that fell down past her hips. The blouse had big billowy sleeves and it was trimmed at the neck with silver. Issie also had silver wristbands to wear.

There was a knock at the door and Amber passed in a pair of shiny black patent leather riding boots. "You're a size seven foot – right?" Issie nodded.

Amber looked at Issie with a stern expression. "It all looks good on you," she said. "I don't think it will need any adjustments at all. Put the boots on and I'll just grab one last thing…"

Issie pulled on the boots. The costume fitted her all right – but she still didn't feel like a Palomino Princess. She felt like Issie Brown in a silly costume. There was another knock at the door and Amber came back in. This time she held a long blonde wig in her hand.

"Let's slip this on you now and see how you look," Amber smiled. She wound Issie's long dark hair back into a twist and pinned it at the back of her head with hair grips. "We'll do this properly on the day of the shoot – this is just to see how it looks," Amber explained. She yanked the blonde wig firmly down on to Issie's head and tucked a couple of stray dark hairs back underneath the blonde fringe.

"Perfect!" Amber said. "Come out and take a look!" Issie walked out of the changing cubicle and stood in front of Amber's full-length mirror.

"Wow! I look amazing!" she gasped.

"You look great!" Amber agreed, fussing round Issie, straightening the hem of her blouse. She stood back and admired her work. "Maybe we'll go with a slightly longer wig? I'll see what we have in stock. Anyway, I'll just get the others to pop out and we can see what you all look like together."

One by one, Stella, Kate and Natasha all emerged from their changing cubicles. Amber had tucked Stella's red hair and Kate's short blonde bob underneath long blonde wigs just like Issie's. Natasha, who didn't need a wig, had undone her plaits so that her own long blonde hair was loose around her shoulders. The three girls were all wearing sky-blue jodhpurs too, but Stella wore a violet blouse, Kate emerald green and Natasha wore scarlet.

"Wow! You guys look incredible!" Issie said.

"I know!" Stella shrieked. "It's so cool!"

"You can take your costumes off now," Amber said, gesturing towards the changing cubicles. "I'm just going to pop out for a coffee. Head over to Helen next door in make-up when you're done."

Stella, Kate, Natasha and Issie all piled back into their cubicles and began carefully taking off their costumes.

"Hey!" Stella called out. "Do you think we'll get to keep our outfits after the movie is finished?"

"I don't think so!" Kate said.

"How about the wigs?" Stella continued. "They must let us keep the wigs. I'm going to ask if we can."

"Stella! Don't—" Issie stopped in mid-sentence as she heard the front door of the costume trailer swing open. The girls fell silent at the sound of a voice outside the trailer. It was a familiar voice. And so loud! Angelique Adams was positively screaming down her mobile phone as she walked into the costume trailer.

"Malcolm? Where the heck have y'all been?" Angelique shouted down the phone. "I've been trying to reach y'all for, like, a whole day! You're my agent!

Never, ever, ever switch off your phone!" There was silence for a moment as Angelique listened to the voice on the other end of the phone.

"Listen, Malcolm. I don't care about any of that. I want to talk about *The Palomino Princess*. It's a nightmare, Malcolm! You've got to get me off this film." There was more silence for a moment as Angelique listened again.

"Malcolm! I can't do this. I thought I could fake it, but I'm so scared. They're going to find out the truth sooner or later and when they do it will be a scandal! Malcolm, you have to get me out of here. I don't know how much longer I can keep this up. Malcolm?" Angelique sounded like she was going to cry.

"Malcolm, I can't talk any more right now. I'm relying on you. Get me off this film before they find out my secret. Do it or you're fired!" Angelique snapped the mobile phone shut just as Amber walked back in the door.

"Hi, Angelique!" she looked around. "Are the girls in here with you?"

Angelique looked puzzled. "What girls?"

"The stunt riders," Amber said. She looked around again and shrugged. "I guess they must have gone to make-up already."

"Yeah, what-ever," Angelique sighed.

Amber gave her a broad smile. "It's so great to be working with you. I've got your costumes all ready…"

Angelique shook her head. The phone call with her agent had left her frazzled. "Uh-uh, no way. I don't have time for this now. My masseuse is waiting for me back at my trailer. All this work is so exhausting!"

"But, Miss Adams!" Amber was panicking now. "I have to fit you for your gowns… Miss Adams?"

"OK then, you can bring them to my trailer. I'll try them on later." Angelique turned on her heels. "Well? Come on then! What are you waiting for?" she shouted at Amber. "And don't even think about bringing anything ugly. I can tell by what you're wearing that you have no taste!"

"Wow! What a brat!" Amber muttered under her breath as she grabbed an armful of dresses off the hanger by the door and raced off after Angelique. "Miss Adams!" she called out. "Miss Adams, wait! I've got the dresses… Miss Adams?" Amber chased after Angelique, leaving the trailer in total silence.

A whole minute later Stella finally stuck her head out, looking about nervously and checking if the coast was clear.

"Hey, you guys! It's safe!" she hissed to the others. "You can come back out now." One by one the other girls emerged from their changing rooms.

"What was that whole scene about?" Kate said, pulling off her blonde wig. "Why doesn't Angelique want to do the movie all of a sudden?"

"She said she was scared," Natasha shrugged. "Maybe someone is blackmailing her or something."

"Ohhh, ohhh! Yes!" Stella said excitedly. "I saw that in a movie once! I bet this sort of thing happens all the time to Hollywood stars. You heard what she said to that Malcolm guy on the phone. She said it would be a scandal if her secret got out!"

"OK, we don't really know what we heard, do we?" Issie began. "I mean maybe we got the wrong end of the stick. We couldn't even hear what he was saying to her on the other end of the phone."

"Maybe not," Stella said. "But I know what we heard. Angelique Adams wants to get off this movie. And she has a secret – a secret that no one knows about." Stella looked at the others. "No one… except us!"

Chapter 6

That night the girls got their chance to try and find out Angelique's secret. When they arrived at the dining hall for dinner Angelique was already there, and she was sitting at a table all by herself. "Well, almost by herself," Stella said, "if you don't count her bodyguard, her assistant and her make-up guy."

"We need to go and sit with her," Issie said decisively. "It's the only way to ask her questions and find out what's going on."

"Oh, really," sneered Natasha. "And what are you going to do? Just fill your plates up at the buffet and sit down with her? Cool."

"Come on, Natasha," Stella said. "Are you doing this with us or not?"

As they approached Angelique's dining table, their plates groaning with prawn risotto and salad, things were going smoothly. Until Angelique's massive bodyguard got up to block their path.

"Miss Adams don't wanna be disturbed," the guard said in a low growl.

"It's OK, Joe." Angelique waved him away with her hand. "They can sit with me." Joe sat back down reluctantly and Issie, Kate, Stella and Natasha all hurriedly grabbed a seat at the table before he changed his mind.

"Ummm, we're the palomino stunt riders. We met yesterday?" Issie said.

Angelique looked at her totally blankly. "What-ever," she said flatly.

"Ummm, yeah, well…" Issie stuttered, trying to stay cool. "Anyway, my Aunt Hester is the head trainer and tomorrow we're going to be riding the horses through a desensitising course…"

"We saw you on E! You know, talking about how you love horses?" Stella blurted out. "So we thought maybe you'd like to come to the stables with us tomorrow…"

Angelique gave a sigh. "Y'know, I really don't think so." Her voice was dripping with boredom. "I've got, like, a totally busy day." She looked at her hands.

"Like, I've totally, absolutely *got* to get a manicure."

"I know what you mean!" Natasha said brightly. "I am so over my nail colour right now!"

Natasha held out her hands for Angelique to see. The Teen Drama Queen peered at Natasha's fingers and for the first time since the girls had sat down she perked up a little. "Hey!" she said. "You're wearing Power Poppy Pink! That is so rad! It used to be totally my fave nail colour."

Natasha nodded. "I know, me too. But now I love Ultra…"

"Ultra-Violet by MAC!" Angelique finished her sentence for her. "That's what I always wear! Wow, you have great taste!"

Natasha looked at her chipped nails. "I know. I get a manicure every week, but horse riding always totally ruins it. I keep telling Mummy I should give up riding and then my nails would look good all the time, but she keeps buying me these expensive ponies…"

"That is so *awful* for you!" Angelique looked genuinely upset at this. She reached over and grabbed Natasha by the hand. "Hey, I know what we can do! I have two beauty therapists working for me back at my trailer. Why don't you come with me tomorrow after breakfast and we can both get a manicure at the same time? We can hang out and stuff."

"She can't!" Stella interrupted. "She has to come with us. We've got training to do."

Natasha glared at Stella. "I can get a manicure first!" she snapped. "Training isn't until the afternoon."

"But, Natasha, you're rostered on for dung duty, remember?" Stella objected.

Angelique smiled. "Hey, hey. I think y'all are forgettin' something, girlfriend," she said in a sarcastic tone. "I am the star here – and I decide." She turned to her assistant. "Debbie, go down to the arena right now and tell that trainer lady that Natasha is going to be too busy for her chores tomorrow. Tell her she's hanging out with me."

"Well!" Stella groaned as the girls walked back to the barracks after dinner. "That kind of backfired, didn't it? We're supposed to be finding out Angelique's secret – not her favourite nail colour!"

Natasha glared at Stella. "Oh, this is so typical! You're just jealous because Angelique wants to be my friend – not yours. I'm so over you and your attitude, Stella. I don't want anything to do with your stupid spying on Angelique anyway – find out her secret yourself if you're so smart!" She stomped off ahead in a huff leaving Stella, Kate and Issie behind.

"Jealous? As if I would be jealous of her!" Stella grumbled. "Just because she thinks Angelique Adams is her NBF! Stupid Stuck-up Tucker. I am so sick of her! Aren't you, Issie? Issie?"

Issie wasn't listening. She was deep in her own thoughts, thinking about their first riding session tomorrow. While Natasha was hanging out with Angelique, maybe it was time for her to make a new friend too. Tomorrow she was going to make a start with Stardust.

Issie woke up early the next morning and decided to skip breakfast and go straight to the stables.

"There is no better way to get to know a horse than with a body brush and a curry comb in your hand," Tom Avery always said. It was true. After all, hadn't Issie bonded with Blaze by grooming and caring for the chestnut mare? Issie loved grooming Blaze. She would spend hours and hours brushing her pony. Even now that Blaze was heavily pregnant she would still groom her every day, even if she wasn't riding her. Her favourite part was brushing out Blaze's gorgeous flaxen tail until it floated behind her like spun sugar candy. Blaze's favourite part was having the soft body brush used on her face just beneath her forelock. The mare would shut her eyes and go into a trance as Issie brushed her gently.

Issie looked at her grooming kit. She had packed everything neatly, including a rubber massage mitt which Blaze just loved. Hopefully Stardust would love it too. When she reached the stables, Stardust was standing with her head out over the top of the Dutch door. When she saw Issie coming though, she pulled her head back in and went to the furthest corner of her stall, making it clear that she wasn't keen on company.

"Hey, girl," Issie said softly as she opened the door to the loose box and walked in. She shouldered the halter she had brought with her, pulled a carrot out of her gilet pocket and offered it to the golden mare.

Stardust looked at the carrot, but she didn't move. Issie, too, stayed rooted to the spot. Finally, after a minute or so, Issie could see that Stardust wasn't going to budge. The game of wills had been played and Issie had lost. She stepped forward towards the mare and Stardust gave her a doleful look as she took the carrot out of Issie's hand.

"Good girl, Stardust, good girl," Issie cooed as she slipped the lead rope around Stardust's neck and began buckling up the halter over the mare's head. "I can see we're gonna get along just fine... owww!"

Stardust, who had finished her carrot, had made a sudden lunge forward as Issie was doing up the halter and managed to land a nasty nip on Issie's upper arm!

Issie squealed, letting go of the lead rope and grabbing at her sleeve. She instinctively stepped back from the palomino who was still glaring at her with her ears flat back.

"Stardust!" a voice over the Dutch door called out. Issie turned and saw Aidan standing there.

"Did she get you?" There was concern in Aidan's voice as he unbolted the door and dashed over to check on her.

"I, I don't think it's too bad," Issie said, trying desperately not to cry. "Aidan, I wasn't even doing anything! I was just trying to do up her halter and..."

"I know," Aidan said. "Believe me. It's not you. She's the same with everyone. She's tried to bite me loads of times." He rolled up the sleeve of Issie's shirt and checked her arm where Stardust had struck.

"You're lucky. She hasn't broken the skin. It's not a bad one," he said.

"It feels bad enough," Issie groaned.

"Come out of here for a minute and get your breath back," Aidan said, putting his arm round Issie and leading her out of the loose box. He sat down with her on a bale of hay. "She's been like that ever since she arrived at our stables," Aidan said. "I can't figure it out. Hester says she's a real star. She's done three movies already this year, but I can't get her to behave at all and I don't know what's wrong with her."

"Will Aunty Hess really get rid of her if she's no good?" Issie said. "Natasha said something. She was probably just being stupid but she said maybe Stardust would go to the glue factory."

Aidan shook his head. "I don't know. Hester doesn't own Stardust. It's up to her owners what happens to her." He looked at Issie. "You've got to remember that Stardust isn't a pony-club pony, she's a working horse. Movies are what she does and if she can't work as a stunt horse any more then I don't imagine that anyone is going to bother to pay for her upkeep."

Even though Stardust had just bitten her, Issie felt sick at the idea of something awful happening to the palomino.

"Hester is right then," she said. "You and me, we have to figure her out. We've got to get her to behave herself so she doesn't get kicked off this movie."

Aidan smiled at Issie. "What do you mean 'we'? You're the horse whisperer here. You'll figure her out, just like you did with Destiny."

"That was different!" Issie protested.

"He misses you, you know," Aidan said, looking at Destiny's stall. The big black horse had his head out over the top half of the door and was watching them.

"What do you mean?" Issie was confused.

"Destiny," Aidan said. "He misses you. After you left Blackthorn Farm, he kept trotting up and down the fenceline for days. He wouldn't settle down. It was as if he was waiting for you to come back again." Aidan looked at Issie. She was startled by how blue and intense his eyes were.

"Me too," he said softly.

"What?"

"I've missed you, Issie."

Issie felt her tummy doing flip-flops. "I, uhhh… ummm…" She felt Aidan's hand gently reaching out to take her own. He leant closer and Issie could feel his fringe against her cheek, tickling her skin.

"Hey!" Stella's voice shocked her back to reality. "There you both are! I've been looking for ages. Come on! Hester is here. We're ready to start the training session."

Issie felt the butterflies in her tummy churning up once more. Not the nice kind of butterflies that she had got when Aidan held her hand at the stables. No, these butterflies were doing nervous flip-flops in her belly until she felt sick. Issie hated feeling like this. She knew she would only pass her nerves on to her horse, but she couldn't help it. Now here they were all saddled up in the arena. She would be riding Stardust for the first time.

"We need to get straight into the desensitising work," Hester said to the girls as they walked across the sawdust floor of the arena. "Rupert, the director, wants us ready to be on the set with the palominos by next week. He's heard the rumours about the trouble we've been having with Stardust and I want to prove to him that the Daredevil Ponies are ready for action."

"Who are the Daredevil Ponies?" Issie looked confused.

"We are! That's the name of my stunt horse company – the Daredevil Ponies. Chase scenes, battle scenes, stampedes – there's no stunt that's too wild or too dangerous for my daredevils." Hester smiled. "Now let's get training, shall we?" She handed the girls helmets and back protectors. "Put these on please. When you're doing the stunts for the cameras you'll have to ride without any helmets. But at practice time we always wear them."

Stella wasn't paying attention though. She was busy staring at the curious set-up in the middle of the arena. "What's all that junk?" she asked.

"Stella, that's not junk," Hester grinned. "That is a crucial part of your film training. It's an obstacle course. These ponies will encounter many strange situations when we're filming and I've tried to recreate the same obstacles here in the training arena," Hester said. "They need to be bombproof – they must not bolt or shy or buck no matter what distractions we throw at them. We'll take them through the course here and see if they have any weaknesses that we need to work on."

Hester strode over to the middle of the arena. "At the start of the course, I want each of you to canter over to the centre of the arena and grab your sword out of the box here without getting off your horse." She pointed to the broadswords, which were facing blade downwards with their handles sticking out of the tea chest in the middle of the arena. "They're not real of course; they're made of hardwood," she said, picking one up and waving it about expertly.

"Then you ride back over here." Hester strode over to a big pile of black blankets. "This is obstacle number one. You must make your horses stand perfectly still while Aidan and I flap these at you. The vampire riders wear big black capes that billow in the breeze – so your horses need to become accustomed to black flappy things in their faces."

The second obstacle was a row of bending poles surrounded by big lights, which were set up at blinding angles and kept flashing on and off. "You have to wind your way through the poles, teaching the horses to ignore the lights," Hester said. "They must get used to the bright lighting on the film set."

The last obstacle was a row of straw dummies which had been strapped on to poles with bullseyes painted on their hessian-sack chests.

"Now this one is fun! You line up here, then ride straight at the dummy with your weapon held high and thrust it into his chest to hit the bullseye!" Hester looked at the girls. "We'll do it at a canter today and work up to a gallop by the end of the week."

"A gallop!" Stella squeaked. "So when we do this for real in the movie we'll be galloping with no helmets?"

"Well, yes, poppet." Hester smiled at her. "You're stunt riders. What did you think you'd be doing? This isn't a pony-club games day, sweetie. This is daredevil stuff!"

Stella's face turned pale. "But I've never even used a sword..."

Hester laughed. "Stella! You're on Paris. She knows exactly what to do. She's been well trained. She'll never put a hoof wrong, I promise you." Hester saw the uncertain looks on her riders' faces. "Right then! Issie, why don't you start? Go ahead on Stardust and show them how it's done."

Issie's butterflies were positively doing cartwheels now as she clucked Stardust forward and stood in front of everyone at the start of the course.

"Right then," Hester said, "canter Stardust to the tea chest and get your sword."

This was easier said than done. Stardust didn't seem to want to canter. The mare had her ears back in a grumpy mood and the most she would do was trot over to the tea chest. Then, when they reached the box, Stardust shivered and snorted and refused to get close enough for Issie to take a sword out.

"Stardust! What's wrong?" Issie gave the mare a tap with her heels, but instead of responding and moving forward, Stardust began to fret and pace about on the spot. She wasn't listening to Issie at all.

"Aidan," Hester said, "run over there, would you, and grab a sword out for Issie?" Aidan nodded and set off at a jog across the sawdust arena. He reached the box and pulled out one of the wooden broadswords. Then he walked over to Stardust, who was now backing away from him and trembling, and passed the sword up so that Issie could grasp the handle.

Issie had barely a moment to feel the weight of the sword in her hand before everything went bad. Suddenly, without any warning, Stardust went straight up on her hind legs and reared, flinging Issie backwards out of the saddle. Issie instantly dropped the sword and grabbed with both hands for Stardust's mane as the mare rose up on her hindquarters, thrashing her legs in the air.

"Hold on!" Aidan yelled as he came running back towards her to help.

Issie clung on for dear life. What else could she do? By the time Aidan reached her side, Stardust landed back down on the ground with Issie as white as a sheet.

"Ohmygod! Stardust!" Issie was shaking with shock.

But before she could gather her wits – and her reins – Stardust began to perform her next trick. The golden palomino dropped suddenly to her knees. "Stardust!" Issie shrieked. She had been ready for the mare to misbehave, but she hadn't been expecting anything like this. Stardust was still on her knees and was ignoring Issie's frantic kicks. "Get up, Stardust!" Issie growled.

"Hoi hoi! Up, girl!" Aunt Hester barked at the mare as she ran forward to help. But Stardust ignored Aidan and Hester and kept lowering herself so that she was now almost lying down on her side.

"Jump!" Hester yelled at Issie. "Isadora – jump! Do it now!"

Issie suddenly realised the danger she was in. Stardust was about to roll on top of her! If she didn't leap off now, she would be crushed beneath the weight of the enormous horse. Instinctively, she threw herself into the air, flying sideways out of the saddle. She managed to land clear of Stardust, falling hard to the ground and inhaling a mouthful of sawdust from the arena floor. Sputtering and coughing, she dragged herself up to her knees, quickly crawling on all fours to get out of the palomino's way. She was just in time before Stardust crashed to the ground right beside her and then began to roll.

"Stardust!" Issie squealed as she felt Hester's hands wrap around her waist and drag her out of harm's way.

"Nothing broken?" Hester asked.

"I'm OK," Issie nodded. "Aunty Hess – why did she do that? It was like she did it on purpose…" Issie looked at Stardust who was now rolling back and forth with her legs thrashing the air. There was an awful crack as she rolled right over on her saddle.

"That's the tree broken. That saddle is ruined!" Hester said as she helped Issie to stand up. "Still, thank God you're OK!" She dusted the sawdust off Issie's back. "I really don't know what has got into that mare—"

"Hello, Hester! Everything going well?" a voice suddenly boomed across the arena.

Issie and the others had been so busy with Stardust that they hadn't noticed a scruffy man with dark glasses and a beard walking towards them. The man was accompanied by a girl, also in dark glasses and jeans, with her hair tied back in a bandana.

"Rupert! Oh… ahh… What a surprise!" Hester faltered. "We weren't expecting you until tomorrow…"

"I know." The man took off his sunglasses as he came closer. "I wasn't going to be on set until then, but I ran into Angelique." He gestured to the girl next to him and

Issie finally realised that it was Angelique Adams – almost unrecognisable in her dark glasses and a scarf. She looked sulky, but she gave a reluctant smile when Rupert cast a glance in her direction.

"So, when I heard that you guys were rehearsing I thought, *Hey, why not drop by with Angelique?* It's a great chance for her to meet the palominos."

Hester tried to smile at this. "Uh-huh," she said weakly. "Well, we're right in the middle of rehearsals at the moment…"

"I can see that. And this is Stardust, right?"

"Yes."

"Well then – let's get started!" Rupert smiled. Then he turned to Issie. "You don't mind if Angelique takes Stardust for a ride, do you?"

Issie felt her heart race. What could she say? What could she do to stop this happening? If Angelique got on Stardust now, it would be a disaster!

"Ummm… uh…"

"Excellent!" Rupert said. "Angelique, my superstar rider, this is your moment. Let's get you up on this horse! We're all dying to see you ride!"

Chapter 7

What a disaster! Angelique mustn't ride Stardust! Not now. Issie had been lucky to escape without being injured – but what if the Hollywood superstar wasn't so lucky? They couldn't risk it. They had to stop her – but how?

Issie turned to Aunt Hester. She could see that her aunt was thinking the same thing, both of them desperately searching for a way to prevent disaster.

"I... the thing is..." Issie began. But before she could finish she was interrupted.

"Rupert! What a great idea!" Angelique smiled. "I would love to ride." She paused and pushed her sunglasses back on to her headscarf, locking her violet eyes on the director. "But I think the hair and make-up department are expecting me back for a make-up check. Can we do it tomorrow instead?"

Rupert smiled. "Hey, Angelique, of course! Whatever you say."

"Fabulous!" Angelique purred. "Really – I can't wait. I just love horses sooo much, I can't wait to get ridin'." She shot Stardust a nervous glance and then pushed her sunglasses back down again. "Alrighty," she said, heading for the arena entrance. "Well, I better get to make-up. I'll see y'all later, OK?"

"See you later, Angelique – come and see Hester for a training session tomorrow, OK?" Rupert said.

"For sure!" Angelique grinned as she headed out of the arena gate.

Rupert turned his attention to Issie. "I'm sorry, I don't believe we've met yet. I should have introduced myself earlier. I'm Rupert Conrad, the director of this movie. And you are?" He put out his hand for her to shake.

"Issie, ummm… I mean Isadora Brown," Issie said nervously. "I'm Hester's niece. I'm one of the stunt riders." Issie pointed to her friends standing beside her with their palominos. "And this is Stella, Natasha and Kate. They're all stunt riders too."

Rupert stood and looked Issie up and down. Then he held his hands together in front of his face and made a square with his fingers, closing one eye and squinting at Issie through the hole. He shook his head. "You're not one of the stunt riders," he said firmly.

"I'm not?" Issie said.

"No," Rupert said. "You are much more than that. You… are Angelique Adams's stunt double!"

"What?"

"Hester, your niece is perfect!" Rupert said. "With a blonde wig and a bit of make-up no one will be able to tell her and Angelique apart." He put his hand on Issie's shoulder. "Tell Amber in the costume department that you're the one. When you report to make-up tomorrow before the shoot, get her to dress you as Galatea, OK?"

"OK," Issie said. She was hoping Rupert would take his hand off her shoulder before he noticed that she was shaking with nerves. A few minutes ago she had been scrambling about on her belly in the sawdust trying not to get rolled on by a horse that could crush her to death, and now here she was being cast as a stunt double for the world's most famous teenager! Could this day get any crazier?

"Don't get too excited about this," Rupert added. "There may not be much riding in it for you. As you probably know, Angelique is a great rider – she'll be doing most of her own stunts. You'll probably just be watching from the sidelines."

Rupert clapped his hands together decisively. "Well, that's settled! Excellent."

He turned to Hester. "I was planning on hanging about a bit longer to see you all rehearse, but I'm already behind schedule. I've got a meeting with my special-effects team now. Would you mind if we left it at that for the day?"

"Of course!" Hester said, trying not to sound too relieved. "We wouldn't want to hold you up!"

"Nice to meet you, girls." Rupert waved to Stella, Kate and Natasha. "And you, my new stunt double!" He smiled at Issie.

As Rupert left the arena, Stella couldn't keep quiet any longer. "Ohmygod, Issie, are you OK? You could have been killed! Stardust went totally crazy on you!"

"Stella's right," Hester agreed. Her face was grave. "I'm sorry, Isadora. I knew this mare was trouble, but I had no idea she would do that. I taught her that rolling trick and now she's using it to get rid of her rider. You could have been crushed underneath her if you hadn't leapt off in time."

Issie looked at her aunt. "You mean you taught Stardust how to roll like that?"

Hester nodded. "Her owners had already schooled her in all the classic tricks. I showed her a few new ones, like the rolling. I use the same cues with Diablo to make him lie down and play dead. Stardust is a fast learner. She's so smart she can pick up a new trick like that almost instantly. But those tricks have become dangerous now she's acting like this."

"Aunty Hess, maybe it was my fault," Issie said. "Could it have been something I did that triggered Stardust's behaviour?"

"Yes, well… I suppose that's possible," Hester said. "Stardust's not as push-button as one of my own horses like Diablo or Paris. She's had other trainers and they may have used different cues to make her perform. Perhaps we're giving her the wrong signals."

Hester looked warily at the palomino mare. "Issie, I think we'd better call it a day for you. Why don't you take Stardust back to her loose box while I run the others quickly through the obstacle course?"

Issie was only too happy to agree. She'd had quite enough of Stardust's strange behaviour for one day. Even walking the mare back to the stall made Issie nervous. Stardust had her ears flat back the whole time and Issie had to keep an eye on her in case she tried to bite again.

As she put Stardust back in her stall and took off the crushed saddle with its broken tree, Issie felt sick; she could have been crushed beneath the palomino too. She felt so nervous around Stardust, she was tempted to leave her without even bothering to groom her. Reluctantly she picked up a body brush and began to brush the mare where her saddle had been. As Stardust met Issie's eyes with a cold stare she realised the truth. *I have no trust in her. We've got no bond.*

Issie shook her head. She was being negative. This was silly. Of course they didn't have a bond yet. She had only just met this horse. OK, Stardust may not have been exactly friendly so far, and OK, they hadn't got off to a great start. But surely the whole rearing and rolling incident had been a big misunderstanding? Stardust was a stunt horse after all. Issie had probably given her the wrong signals by mistake and that had caused her to act up. They would get used to each other. All they needed was time.

Issie had given Stardust her hard feed and was brushing the last of the sawdust out of the mare's mane when Natasha stuck her head over the Dutch door of the stall.

"What's taking you so long? We're all waiting for you, you know," Natasha sighed. "The rest of us are ready to go back up to the barracks now, but Stella said we have to wait for you."

"Yeah, just give me a minute," Issie said. She hurriedly put on Stardust's cover, aware that Natasha was glaring at her with contempt the whole time. As if she didn't have enough problems! Now Natasha was annoyed with her for some reason.

The walk home to the barracks was super-painful. Stella wouldn't shut up about how lucky Issie was to be picked as Angelique Adams's stunt double and Natasha wouldn't stop sulking.

"I can't believe Rupert asked you. You're so lucky, Issie!"

"Stella!" Issie groaned. "How am I lucky? If I'm Angelique's stunt double then I'll have to ride Stardust. And you saw what she just did to me! You were right! I could have been killed."

When they finally reached the barracks, Issie headed for her room. She was desperate to lie down, stick her head under her pillow and forget about everything. Unfortunately, Natasha had other plans. She followed Issie into their room and slammed the door behind her. Then she took off her riding boots and threw them noisily into the closet and began to stomp about the room, harrumphing and bristling as she rearranged her teddy bear and hot-water bottle on her bedspread. When Issie reached for the copy of *PONY Magazine* on their dressing table, Natasha shot her a filthy look.

"I was going to read that!" She grabbed it back.

"It's my magazine!" Issie said, snatching at it.

"You know what your problem is?" Natasha snapped at her. "You're not used to sharing anything. You're a spoilt only child who gets everything – and you always get your own way. And now…" Natasha fumed "…now you get to be Angelique Adams's stunt double when it should be me!"

"What?" Issie was stunned.

"It should be me!" Natasha yelled at her. "Angelique is my best friend, not yours! Besides, I look more like her than you do. I even have long blonde hair! I'm just as good a rider as you are, Isadora! Why do you always get to do everything?" She threw the copy of *PONY Magazine* across the room at Issie.

"Here!" she snapped. "You take it. You always get everything in the end anyway – so just go ahead and take it!"

"Natasha, I know you're having a hard time right now because of your mum and dad…" Issie began.

The look on Natasha's face turned to thunder. "I

knew I shouldn't have told you about that!" she shouted. "I suppose you've told Stella and Kate? I know you all talk about me. You're just horrible!" And with that, Natasha stormed out of the room and slammed the door behind her.

Issie sat down on her bed and reached for the crumpled copy of *PONY Magazine*. Her hands were shaking again after Natasha's little screaming session. She hadn't told Stella and Kate anything! And did Natasha really think that Issie had stolen away her chance to stunt-double for Angelique on purpose, just to make her miserable? Issie shook her head. Natasha was nuts. As if it wasn't bad enough having to ride psycho Stardust in this movie – now her room-mate hated her for it.

The door to Issie's room creaked open and Stella stuck her head around it. "Is it safe to come in?" she asked. Issie nodded and Stella came in, followed by Kate.

"What was that about? We heard her yelling from all the way down the hall," Kate said.

Issie told the girls what Natasha had said – minus all the stuff about her parents of course.

"Ohmygod, she is such a stuck-up brat!" Stella said. "Does she really think she's best friends with Angelique? As if! Natasha just wants everything her own way. That's why she can't stand it that you're going to be Angelique's stunt double instead of her."

Issie shook her head in disbelief. "She was just so angry at me. It's not my fault that Rupert picked me!"

"Of course it's not your fault!" Kate said. "Natasha just can't help herself. She doesn't know how to be nice. Forget about it." She gave Issie a hug. "Do you want to move into our room with us?"

Issie felt a hot tear making its way down her left cheek. She rubbed it away angrily with her sleeve. "No. I mean thanks and all that, but no. It'll just make things worse if she thinks I've moved out and we've all ganged up on her."

Kate nodded. "You're right. We'll just leave her alone and let her calm down. I'm sure she'll get over it."

Natasha, however, seemed in no hurry to get over things at all. She spent the rest of the evening ignoring everyone and watching TV, and when it was time to go to the dining hall for dinner she promptly left without them. The girls arrived at the buffet to find that Natasha had already filled her plate and was sitting at a table by herself.

"Should we sit with her?" Issie asked.

"Too late for that," Stella said as Angelique Adams and her entourage walked into the dining hall. Angelique waved at Natasha and made a beeline for her table with her assistant, Tony the make-up artist and Eugene and Bob all trailing along behind her. Issie watched as Eugene circled round Angelique and Natasha with his camera, filming them as they sat and ate together. Then she saw Natasha smile at Angelique and point over towards Issie and whisper. Angelique giggled and then said something to Eugene who nodded and immediately scurried over towards Issie, Kate and Stella.

"Sorry, girls," he said, "you're ruining my documentary. You'll have to leave."

"What do you mean?" Stella said. "We're just sitting here and eating our dinner."

"Exactly," Eugene said. "You're in the way. I can't film if you're sitting here making Angelique uncomfortable. She told me to ask you to leave."

"Oh, really!" Stella said. "Well, you tell Angelique and her friend Stuck-up Tucker that…"

"Hey, Stella, forget it," Issie said. She wasn't about to start a fight with Natasha and Angelique. She didn't need any more drama today. "We can take our plates back to the barracks and eat there." She picked up her plate to leave. "Let's go."

When they got back to the barracks, though, Issie didn't

bother to finish her dinner. She felt too sick to eat anyway. She couldn't believe she had to get back on Stardust again tomorrow. For the first time ever in her life, Issie found herself dreading the idea of getting on a horse.

"I know how you feel. You had a bad fall," Aunt Hester said when Issie told her about her fears the next morning. "But you know the magic rule when you fall off a horse. You have to get straight back on again."

Except, Issie couldn't help thinking, *except I didn't fall from this horse; she deliberately tried to crush me — that's kind of different.*

They were standing in the middle of the arena, with Stardust tacked up and ready to go. Issie watched as Aunt Hester walked over to the mare and attached a long webbing lunge rein, clipping it on to the bit and running it over the mare's poll and down the other side.

"Before you get on her, let's try putting Stardust through her paces on the lunge rein," Hester said. "Run the stirrups up the leathers, will you, dear?"

Issie slid the irons up on their leathers so that they didn't bounce against the mare's sides and then she stood back as Aunt Hester led Stardust into the centre of the arena.

"Tsk tsk, walk on!" Hester clucked at the palomino to get her moving, and Stardust obeyed her commands, stepping out on the lunge at a brisk walk. The lunge rein was about three metres long. Hester held the end of the rein and her eyes followed the mare as she circled around her.

"Trot on!" Hester called out and again Stardust immediately obliged, breaking into a trot on command.

"She's got the most lovely trot!" Issie called out to her aunt.

"That's nothing, wait until you see her canter," Hester grinned. "Come on, Stardust, canter on!"

Hester was right. Stardust had a canter that almost seemed to float above the ground – she was as graceful as a ballerina. Issie could see why Rupert had cast this mare in his movie. With her silver mane and tail flowing out behind her, she looked exactly like the sort of pony that belongs to a princess. Stardust shook her mane and arched her neck, as if she knew that she was the centre of attention as she circled round and round the arena.

"And steady… walk on! And… halt!" Hester instructed. Stardust did just as she was asked, pulling up on the lunge and stopping in front of Hester in a perfect square halt.

"Good girl, Stardust!" Hester said, walking forward and giving the mare a slappy pat on her glossy neck. "Ready to get on her now then?" she asked her niece.

"What, now?" Issie squeaked.

"It's OK," Hester said, running the stirrups back down the leathers. "I'll keep her on the lunge rein. She'll be under my control."

Issie nodded. "All right."

"I'll give you a leg up," Hester said, holding out a hand. Issie put her knee into Hester's palm and her aunt gave her a boost up on to Stardust's back.

"OK?" Hester said. "Let's go."

As Hester led Issie and Stardust back into the centre of the arena, Issie realised that something was missing. The tea chest full of wooden swords was gone.

"Yes, the props department needed it back apparently. You'll have to ride the obstacle course without a sword today, I'm afraid," Hester said.

"I'm going to do the obstacle course?" Issie felt the panic rising in her.

"Not yet. Don't worry, we'll make sure she's well warmed up on the lunge first," Hester said gently. She stood in the centre of the arena and Issie rode Stardust out so that she was at the full length of the lunge rein, walking in a circle round Aunt Hester.

"Trot on!" Hester called out. Issie didn't even need to do anything. She just sat in the saddle while the palomino responded to Hester's voice. Stardust stepped out in a floating trot, her neck arched and her tail swishing. "She seems very happy and you look perfect on her!" Hester called out to Issie with a grin. Issie realised she was grinning too. She felt her nerves melt away with each stride. Stardust was so lovely to ride; it was like being on a cloud.

"Canter!" Hester called, and Stardust obediently rose up into an easy canter. It felt as smooth as a rocking horse. They did a few more circles in each direction at the canter and the trot before Hester pulled Stardust to a halt in the centre of the ring.

"Good girl!" Issie said, giving the mare a hearty slap. "Good Stardust!" She had a smile from ear to ear.

"Well," Hester said, looking pleased, "that went very well. She seems to have settled down with you now. Maybe you're right, Issie, perhaps there was some trigger that made her misbehave yesterday."

Hester looked at her watch. "I was expecting Angelique to turn up for training," she shrugged. "Looks like she isn't coming – and it might be just as well! That gives us time to take Stardust through the obstacle course. We don't have to of course. We could leave it until tomorrow. Filming doesn't start until next Monday so we've still got a day or so to get her ready…"

"No, you haven't! Not any more. There's no time!" A voice across the other side of the arena startled them. Issie and her aunt looked up to see Aidan sprinting towards them across the arena. He had been running so hard he was short of breath and it took a moment for him to pull himself together and speak.

"I just saw Rupert at the dining hall," he panted. "He's posted up a new schedule. The crew are furious. He's changed everything. Apparently it's because they're worried about the weather turning bad. There's a storm forecast for next week and they can't afford to be delayed, so they've moved the whole shooting schedule forward instead." Aidan paused once more, crouching over his knees to catch his breath.

"What do you mean he's moved shooting forward?" Hester was confused.

"Rupert's rescheduled everything, including all the scenes with the horses," Aidan said. "He's going to be filming the forest chase scene tomorrow."

"What does that mean?" Issie asked.

"It means," said Aidan, "that Stardust has to be ready to film her big scene first thing in the morning."

Issie couldn't believe it. She had just started to make a breakthrough with Stardust, and now this! Would Stardust be ready to start filming by tomorrow? Issie felt the butterflies in her tummy returning. Stardust was still so unpredictable. Only one thing was certain: Issie had to be prepared for the worst.

Chapter 8

Stella squealed with excitement and threw herself down in the make-up chair.

"Ohmygod! This is so glamorous!" She beamed over at Issie, Kate and Natasha who were in the chairs next to her also having their make-up applied. "I can't believe we're actually on the set of a real movie!"

"Less giggling please, Stella," Hester said. "Don't forget, you're a Daredevil rider now, so act professional!"

"I *am* a professional! I'm a natural movie star!" Stella grinned. "Did you see our grand entrance, Hester?"

Hester groaned. "Trust me, Stella, *everyone* saw that."

The shooting location this morning was a ridge on the farm, not too far from the stables, and Aunt Hester had suggested that the four girls ride the palominos to the set.

She hadn't expected them to gallop up the hill together in a row, whooping and hollering like cowgirls, waving their hands in the air.

"We were just warming up and getting into character!" Stella had pouted when Hester told them off for being irresponsible.

Once they had tethered their palominos to one of the silver crew trucks, the girls were whisked off to have make-up and wigs applied before they got into their costumes. Meanwhile, the rest of the film crew were busily scurrying about the trucks. The girls watched as the men unloaded the lighting rigs, cameras and props.

"All this just for one scene?" Kate said.

"It's not just any scene!" Stella said. "This is the chase in the forest when the princess riders get away from the vampire horsemen. It's one of the most exciting bits in the whole book."

Hester looked over at Issie, who hadn't said anything since the girls had arrived on the set. "You're very quiet, Isadora. Are you OK?"

Issie smiled. "Sure, I'm fine, Aunty Hess."

The truth was she wasn't fine at all. Yesterday's training session had gone well. No, it had been better than that, Stardust hadn't made a single mistake. Issie had even ridden her through the obstacle course and Stardust hadn't put a hoof wrong. Still, even though the palomino seemed to be behaving herself, Issie couldn't help feeling there was something wrong with this horse – as if she was just waiting for the chance to try one of her tricks again.

Issie had really tried to make friends with Stardust. She had spent ages grooming her after their training session and had even smuggled extra carrots and some sugar cubes in her pocket for the mare. But sugar treats weren't going to win Stardust over and deep down in her horsy instincts Issie knew it. Sure, Stardust had stopped trying to bite her, but there was still no bond between them. It was as if Issie was an annoying fly buzzing around and Stardust was just waiting for her chance to flick her tail and swat her away.

"It's like she hates me or something," Issie had told Stella and Kate when she arrived back at the barracks that night.

"You're being ridiculous!" Kate said. "Stardust does not hate you. You know, Issie, you can't expect every horse to be like Blaze. Blaze is special. You saved her life and she loves you because of that, because of everything you've been through together. Stardust doesn't even know you yet. You just need to give her some time, that's all."

Maybe Kate was right, Issie thought. But it didn't matter. There was no time. This was it. They were on the film set and Stardust had to be ready for action. Issie felt a shiver run up her spine. Oh well, the chances were that she wasn't going to be in this scene anyway. Angelique was supposed to be riding Stardust today. Issie would just be standing on the sidelines in her blonde wig, watching along with everyone else.

"Can I have your attention, everyone?" Rupert shouted out. He was standing on top of a camera dolly next to one of the silver trucks and already a large crowd of cameramen and lighting operators, make-up artists and assistants had gathered round him. At the back of the crowd were the vampire riders, all of them mounted up on their black horses. Issie recognised Aidan on a dyed-black Diablo and gave him a wave. He waved back and smiled, revealing a set of fake white vampire fangs.

"Hurry up and come over to join us, please, palomino riders!" Rupert called to the girls. Issie, Stella, Kate and Natasha instantly did as Rupert said, riding their horses over to where the others were standing.

"Right!" he said once everyone was assembled. "Today we're shooting the scene where the vampire riders chase Galatea and her princesses through the forest of Eleria…"

"Where's Princess Galatea then?" Stella whispered to Issie.

The girls looked around. Angelique was nowhere to be seen.

"I think she's still in her trailer," Issie said, pointing to a long silver caravan with the name Angelique Adams on the door in large hot-pink letters.

At that moment, the door swung open and Angelique emerged from her trailer followed by a string of make-up artists, costume people, personal assistants carrying her coffee and mobile phone and, of course, Eugene and Bob, who were circling her like sharks with their camera.

"Good timing, Angelique!" Rupert called to his star. "Come on over! I was just explaining the scene."

Angelique was expressionless behind her dark glasses as she walked towards them. She snapped her fingers at one of her assistants who quickly handed over her coffee. When she saw Issie and the other girls all mounted on their horses, Angelique seemed to falter for a moment. She walked in a wide circle around them, positioning herself at the rear of the crowd as the director spoke.

"OK, as I was saying, here's what we'll be shooting today," Rupert explained. "We'll be doing the whole chase scene as one single take. Angelique, that means that when Francis and his vampires start to chase you and the princesses, you're going to ride right along the ridge ahead of us here, OK? Then the princesses will act as a decoy and lead the vampire riders off to the left. All the vampires will follow the princesses. Except for Francis. He'll stay on your tail. You just keep riding straight ahead along the ridge, weaving through the trees until you reach that large oak – straight past that tree and Aidan will follow you."

Aidan nodded at this and Rupert turned his attention to him. "Aidan, you'll be at the front of the vampire riders. I want you to stay close to Angelique, just a couple of horse lengths behind her. This is the scene where Galatea only just escapes Francis, so when you pass the oak tree and the trees start to get more dense, that's when you make your move. I need you to come right up next to her, so close that you actually touch her. Make a grab for her. We want it to look like she's in real trouble, OK?"

"No problem!" Aidan said cheerfully.

"Excellent. Can we have the camera crews in position and lighting technicians do your checks now, please? I want everybody ready in five minutes for our first run-through," Rupert said.

"You heard him!" the assistant director barked. "Come

on, everyone, let's go! Can the riders mount up, please?"

Rupert glanced over at Issie. "Isadora," he said, "you won't be riding. You can hand Stardust over to Angelique for this scene, thanks."

Issie dismounted from Stardust and began to lead her towards Angelique, ready to hand the reins over to the actress so that she could mount up. When Angelique saw Issie coming towards her, her expression turned sour. Issie smiled and gave a friendly wave as she led the palomino towards her, but Angelique just glared back at her.

Issie was still a few metres away from the Hollywood star when Angelique let out the most bloodcurdling scream.

"Oww! Ohh! Ohhhhhhh!" Angelique yelled.

"What?" Issie was panic-stricken. "What's wrong?"

Angelique flopped down dramatically on the ground, cradling her foot in her hands. Her face was screwed up with pain and she was whimpering pitifully.

"Owwww!" Angelique screamed again. "Rupert! Ohmygod! This... this... idiot here just made the horse stamp on my foot!"

Issie looked at Angelique in amazement. "What?" she said. "But I..."

"Don't say another word!" Angelique shouted at her. "You're a total incompetent. This is so unprofessional! I don't believe it!" She was still clutching her foot and rolling about on the ground.

"Get the doctor!" Rupert shouted at one of his assistants as he raced over to his star's side. "Angelique! Are you OK?"

"No, Rupert," Angelique was sobbing now, "I think... I think it's broken!"

"Quick! Ice packs!" Rupert shouted to another crew member.

"Oh, and can you get me another coffee?" Angelique asked her assistant, pausing suddenly between sobs to order a latte.

As she sat on the ground with the crew gathered around her, Eugene and Bob hovered like vultures with their camera whirring the whole time. "Angel sweetheart! This is great! We're getting terrific footage!" Eugene burbled.

"Eugene! My foot! Show some sympathy!" Angelique snapped. Then, when she realised the camera was still rolling, she looked directly down the lens with a pouty, pained expression. As Eugene came in for a close-up, Angelique allowed a single, solitary tear to trickle down her cheek. Issie couldn't believe what she was seeing.

"But, but I..." she began.

"Hey!" Eugene snapped over his shoulder at her. "Get

that horse out of here! I think you've done enough damage, don't you?"

Bewildered, Issie led Stardust back out of the way of the crowd, over to where Stella, Kate and Natasha were standing.

"What an idiot! I can't believe you let Stardust stand on her foot!" Natasha hissed at Issie.

"I didn't!" Issie hissed back. "I swear. We were nowhere near her! We were miles away and suddenly Angelique just collapsed on the ground and started wailing!"

Angelique's hysterics reached a peak just as the paramedics arrived. "Well," Stella said, "if Stardust didn't stand on her foot then she sure is a great actress!"

The crowd around Angelique had become even bigger now as the paramedics moved her on to a stretcher and began to carry her back to her trailer.

"Angel! No, Angel!" Eugene ran after her, his camera still rolling. Then the little man left Angelique's side and scurried over to Rupert. "This is no good! You gotta make her ride!" Eugene shouted at him. "Strap her foot up! Do what it takes. I need her to ride this scene! I need more drama!"

Rupert stared coolly at Eugene. "She's my star, Eugene, and she's been injured. If she rides now, she may make the injury worse and then she won't be able to work at all."

Eugene rubbed his hands together anxiously. "But, Rupert, you've got to—"

"I don't have to do anything, Eugene," Rupert frowned. "Angelique may have given you permission to get underfoot, trailing her around like a dog to make your behind-the-scenes special, but don't forget that I'm the one who makes the decisions on this movie. You're just a two-bit documentary maker." He turned to Issie.

"Mount up!" Rupert said gruffly. "You've injured my star and now it looks like you're getting rewarded for it – I need you to ride the scene."

"But I didn't…" Issie began to say. But it was too late. Rupert had already turned his back on her and was barking at his crew, yelling at them to get into position.

"Let's move!" he snapped. "Positions, everyone – now!"

"Are you OK, Isadora?" Aunt Hester asked.

"Aunty Hess!" Issie said. "I wasn't even near Angelique! Stardust didn't stand on her foot! I don't know what's happening – this is crazy!"

Hester looked concerned. "Really?" she said. "Well, we'll discuss it later. But right now, Issie, I need you to ride. Are you up for it?"

Issie looked at Stardust. She still didn't trust this horse. All of her horsy instincts screamed out that she shouldn't do this. But after Angelique's drama-queen moment just now, the whole crew was furious with her because they believed that she'd injured the star. If she refused to ride, well, she would get fired for sure, and Aunt Hester probably would be too. Everyone was relying on her. She had no choice.

"I'm fine, Aunty Hess." She gave her aunt a weak smile. "Let's go."

The vampire riders, Issie, Kate, Natasha and Stella all got into position at the start of the ridge track and Rupert ran them through the scene one more time.

"You, Galatea! Keep going at full gallop the entire time. The vampire riders will follow you all the way past those trees to the big oak on the ridge. That's your marker, OK? At the big tree, the rest of the princesses and palominos will turn to the left and lead the vampires away from you. You'll keep on riding into the woods and Aidan will follow at a gallop. That's when he'll gain on you and try to pull you off your horse. You have to swing at him with your sword while you're galloping. OK?"

Issie looked at the ridge they were going to ride along. It was dotted with enormous trees which the riders would need to weave in and out of as they rode. It was easy to tell which one was the big oak because it was twice the size of the others.

"So, I stay in front of the other riders?" Issie asked.

Rupert nodded. "But don't get too far in front or it won't look exciting enough. You must make it look as if it's a matter of life and death." He looked at the riders. "Right then. Everyone ready? Let's do the first take, shall we?"

The riders prepared to gallop on Rupert's command.

"Positions, everyone!" Rupert shouted to his crew.

"Ready to go!" the reply came back.

"All right. Riders ready? On my say-so… and…"

"Hey, hold on! Wait!" There was a shout as a man from the props department ran forward. He was waving a wooden broadsword in his hand. "Sorry, Rupert," he said. "My fault entirely. I almost forgot that Galatea is supposed to be carrying a sword in this scene."

Rupert nodded. "Hurry up and get in there, then, and give it to her."

The props man stepped forward with the broadsword and Issie felt Stardust tense underneath her. The mare stepped backwards nervously and Issie had to hold her tightly so that she could reach down and take the sword from the props man. As they took their positions again,

Issie realised something was wrong. Stardust was trembling, her muscles twitching, her tail swishing anxiously.

"Steady, girl, steady. What's wrong?" Issie's voice was low and soft as she spoke gently to the mare, trying to soothe her. But Stardust wasn't listening and there wasn't any time to calm the mare down.

"Lights!" Rupert called. "Camera and… action!"

The call took Issie by surprise. She had been busy fumbling with her reins trying to figure out how to grip the broadsword and hold back Stardust at the same time. Now, at Rupert's call, Stardust sprang forward like a racehorse from a starting gate, startling Issie so that she was left behind in the saddle. She made a desperate grab at Stardust's mane with one hand to keep her balance, still managing to hold on to the reins and her sword in the other.

"Steady, girl!" Stardust had broken so swiftly when Rupert called action that she was already too far out in front of the other horses. Issie needed to slow the mare down. If Stardust got too far away from Aidan and the vampire riders, it would totally ruin the scene.

Issie hauled back on the reins and for a moment Stardust seemed to slow her stride. Behind her, she could hear the thunder of hooves as Kate, Stella and Natasha galloped after her on their palominos. She turned round to check and saw the girls riding hard, with the black horses and the vampire riders following at their heels. Issie felt a chill run through her as she realised just how dangerous this stunt really was. The other horses were so close behind and galloping so fast that she couldn't afford to make a mistake. If she fell off Stardust right now, she would be directly in their path and they would trample her for sure.

Stardust was in full gallop, still nervous and tense and still fighting hard against Issie's hold on the reins as they galloped along the ridge, winding between the big trees, heading for the giant oak up ahead.

She's too fast, Issie thought. *I have to slow her down.* She pulled back hard on the reins and felt a wave of fear as Stardust completely failed to respond. The mare was bolting! She was bearing down on the bit and leaning hard so that all her strength was fighting against her rider. Issie heaved on the reins again. It felt like her shoulders were being wrenched out of their sockets.

Her hands were aching now, her fingers cramping from holding on to the sword and the reins. To make matters worse, the frothy sweat on the palomino's neck had rubbed into the leather of the reins, making them slick and wet. They were so slippery it was getting harder and harder for Issie to hold on.

Carefully Issie took her left hand off the reins, just for a moment, so that she could wipe her palm dry on her jodhpurs and get a better grip. She was still holding the sword in her other hand, while trying to keep her hold on the reins too, except the leather was just too slippery. As the palomino strained at the bit, Issie felt a sudden panic rising in her as both the leathers slipped clean out of her hands. She had completely lost her reins! Stardust was out of control.

Chapter 9

There is no feeling more terrifying in the whole world than being on a horse that is bolting. Issie made a frantic grab and managed to get the reins back, but by then Stardust had the bit between her teeth. Issie was struggling to hold her back. She could barely even keep a grip on the reins. She felt them sliding again back through her fingers and looked down at the broadsword clasped in her right hand. It would ruin the scene if she dropped it now, but she had no choice. If she was going to stop this runaway horse, she needed both hands to do it.

Issie opened the cramped, closed fingers of her right hand and felt the weight of the big wooden broadsword slip out of her hands. As the sword fell with a clatter to the ground, Stardust spooked, swerving violently to the left, and Issie let out a squeal as she struggled once more to hang on.

Stardust straightened up and Issie regained her balance and sat back in the saddle. She pulled back as hard as she could on both reins but Stardust didn't respond. The palomino was so strong and Issie's arms were so tired, they felt like jelly.

As another tree brushed against her, almost knocking her off her horse this time, Issie could feel the panic rising in her. They were about to reach the oak. Beyond the big tree the woods began to close in and become more dense. It would be harder to navigate her way through them. Riding like this, on a runaway horse at full gallop, there was no way she would be able to steer safely through the trees.

Then suddenly she remembered what Avery had said to her once about what to do when a horse bolts. *If a horse is too strong for you to fight them, the only way to stop is to make them turn.*

That was it! Issie had been fighting the mare by hauling on both reins at once. She couldn't beat Stardust like that. The mare was too powerful, leaning her full weight against Issie's hands with the bit in her teeth, making her virtually impossible to stop. But what would happen if Issie just tried pulling on one rein?

It would mean timing it right. The trees were thick now and she'd have to dodge and weave expertly between them. But what choice did she have? If Stardust kept galloping into the trees at this speed, Issie would be knocked off by a low branch for certain. She had to try something.

Issie ducked as Stardust swept beneath the branches of the giant oak. Then she sat upright and braced herself to turn, taking a deep breath, sitting back in the saddle and pushing her heels down low in the stirrups.

Tom had better be right about this, she thought as she let her right rein slide through her fingers and go completely slack. Then she put all of her strength into her left arm and pulled.

As she heaved on one single rein, the sudden sideways motion yanked the bit clean out from between Stardust's teeth. Surprised, Stardust lurched to the left, and then her stride slowed as she felt the bit against the bars of her mouth once more. Within a few strides, Issie had the horse back under control, slowing her down to a canter, then a trot, then a walk and finally, with relief, she had pulled up to a halt. It had worked!

Issie sat there, exhausted and shaking. Beneath her, Stardust was heaving after the exertion of her wild gallop.

Her flanks were working in and out like bellows and her neck was dripping wet with sweat.

"Issie! Issie! Are you OK?" Aidan, who had been galloping after her all this time, pulled Diablo up next to Stardust. "You were going so fast even Diablo couldn't keep up."

"She bolted, Aidan. She got the bit between her teeth and I tried, but I couldn't stop her," Issie said. She was shaking and her face was pale from shock.

Aidan jumped off Diablo, grasping Stardust's reins. Issie went to dismount too and felt her legs turn to rubber. They could barely hold her and she almost collapsed as she landed on the ground.

"Hey! Easy there, tiger!" Aidan put his arm around her to support her. "Are you OK?"

Issie collapsed in Aidan's arms and as soon as she felt safe the tears started. She was furious with herself for crying like this – and on the film set! She was supposed to be a stunt rider! If the others saw her like this, it would all be so embarrassing!

Suddenly there was the roar of an engine as a big black motorcycle came tearing towards them. Issie couldn't tell who the driver was because of the black visor on his helmet, but she recognised the passenger riding pillion on the back. It was Rupert and he didn't look pleased. His mouth was set in a grim line as he leapt off the back of the motorcycle and ran towards them.

"Hey, hey, what happened? Why did you stop? It was all going so brilliantly!" he said. As he said this, there was the high-pitched whine of another motorcycle belting along the track towards them. It was Bob and Eugene with their camera still whirring and filming.

"What happened?" Eugene demanded as Bob pulled the bike up. "Is anyone hurt?"

Aidan looked at Rupert with dark eyes. "No, we're OK."

"Oh!" Eugene sounded almost disappointed to hear this. He put his camera down. "Well, could you at least pretend you're hurt or something?" he said to Issie in a low voice. "You know, mug it up a bit for the cameras?"

"Leave her alone," Aidan said, pushing Eugene's camera away. "Can't you see she's been through enough?"

"Issie! Issie are you OK?"

Issie looked up to see the panic-stricken face of her Aunt Hester running towards her.

"I'm fine, Aunty Hess," Issie said. "Honestly."

"What on earth went wrong? Why did you drop your sword? Why didn't you follow your cues?" Hester asked.

Issie didn't want to get Stardust into trouble, but she

realised that she had no choice. She had to tell Aunt Hester the truth.

"Aunty Hess, Stardust bolted on me. It happened right at the start and I tried but I couldn't stop her. I was fighting her all the way and she wouldn't listen to me."

Hester gave Issie a hug. "You did very well to stay on and stop her."

"Problems with Stardust?" Rupert asked.

Hester nodded reluctantly.

"I told you, Hester, I don't have time for stunt horses that can't do the job. This little incident has cost us money and a whole day's filming. You're in charge here – I don't want another mistake like this happening again. I think I'm making myself clear?" Rupert's face was like thunder.

He called to his driver, who pulled up next to him so that he could climb back on to the motorcycle. "I'm going back to base. I'll get my assistant to let the crew know that we're wrapped. We can't continue today. We'll pick it up first thing in the morning. And your horses had better be ready next time." They watched as the director sped off on the motorcycle in a cloud of indignation and dust.

"He took that pretty well, didn't he?" Aidan groaned.

Hester sighed. "I'm afraid he's right. The horses are

my responsibility and this was the final straw. I should have made the decision sooner – now I've delayed filming and put lives at risk." Hester paused. "Stardust is just too dangerous and unpredictable to play Seraphine. She'll have to be replaced."

"But Aunty Hess!" Issie was shocked. "Stardust is the perfect Seraphine. Rupert chose her himself! Besides, what will happen to her if we get rid of her? What will her owners do to her if she can't work in the movies any more?"

Hester looked grim. "We can't afford to worry about that, Issie. I have to think of your safety and the safety of the whole cast and crew. Besides, if Stardust keeps acting like this she will ruin the movie. She's badly behaved and I don't know what to do with her. You heard what Rupert said. I'm afraid Stardust leaves us with no choice. She's got to go!"

The girls were already back at the stables waiting anxiously when Issie and Stardust arrived. "Ohmygod! Issie! Are you OK?" Stella didn't wait for her friend to speak. "We heard what Rupert said. Would Hester really get rid of Stardust? She wouldn't, would she? Oh, this is awful!"

"I know," Issie agreed. Even though Stardust had terrified her with her runaway antics, she still didn't want the palomino to get fired from the film. "I wish there was something we could do, but Aunty Hess has made her mind up."

"Do you know why Stardust bolted?" Kate asked.

"I don't know." Issie shook her head.

"It's like this whole film is cursed or something," Stella said, looking spooked.

"Don't be ridiculous, Stella! Stardust bolted, that's all!" Issie snapped.

"Oh yeah?" Stella said. "Well, what about Angelique's foot? Disasters like that don't usually happen on movie sets!"

"But that's just it!" Issie said. "Stardust and I weren't even close to Angelique and she just collapsed on the ground and started yelling about how we'd broken her foot. It was all an act. We didn't do it!"

"So why would Angelique pretend to be hurt?" Kate wondered.

"To get out of making the film of course!" Stella replied. "She said in the changing rooms that she wanted to get out of making this movie – no matter what!"

"So she's willing to pretend she's broken her foot? That sounds—" The girls stopped speaking abruptly as the tack-room door swung open and Natasha walked in.

"Oh," she said frostily, "I see. Another one of your secret meetings I suppose. All the gang together as usual – except me." She turned around to leave.

"Natasha!" Issie called after her. "It's not like that."

"Yes it is," Natasha turned on her. "You've got your little gang. You never include me in anything. It doesn't matter how much I try, I'll never be a part of it. Well, fine, I don't want to be anyway!" And with that she flounced back out of the door, slamming it behind her.

Issie groaned. "Should I go after her?"

"And say what?" Stella said. "She's right. We don't want her in the gang."

"Stella!" Issie said. "Did it ever occur to you that Natasha is such a total cow to us because she feels left out and wants to be our friend, but we never include her?"

"No," Stella said flatly. "No. It really didn't."

Natasha was in a huff with them – the best thing to do was to leave her until she calmed down. As for Angelique: "All we can do is keep an eye on her in case she does anything else suspicious," Hester told Issie when they talked about it a bit later. Issie tried to object but she knew her aunt was right. Rupert would never believe her word over Angelique's.

What would have happened, Issie wondered, if it had been Angelique on Stardust instead of her? Issie kept thinking back to that morning when Stardust bolted. OK, the mare could be super-naughty, but was it just naughtiness that made her bolt? There had to be some pattern to her bad behaviour. If only Issie could figure it out.

When she went to check on the palomino mare in her stall that afternoon, Stardust almost seemed glad to see Issie for once. She even put her head over the stall and nickered at the sight of her.

Issie reached out and stroked the palomino's pretty velvet muzzle and Stardust snuffled her palm, hoping for carrots. Then she rubbed her nose affectionately against Issie's sleeve as if to say, "I'm sorry I caused all that trouble today," which only made Issie feel even worse.

By the time she went to bed that night, Issie was sick with worry. She kept thinking about the chase scene and how she couldn't stop Stardust. The palomino wasn't at all like her beloved Blaze. Perhaps Stella was right – maybe Issie was expecting too much. She couldn't expect to bond with a horse like Stardust the way she had bonded with Blaze. All of this just made her miss Blaze more than ever. She was so homesick for her chestnut mare. Well, it was only one more day until the weekend and then she could go home and see her again.

Issie got her chance to go home for the weekend sooner than she thought. When she arrived at the dining hall for breakfast the next morning, she discovered that Friday's filming schedule had also been abandoned because of Angelique's injured foot.

"Angelique's doctor insists that she needs a week to heal and Rupert says there's no point in filming until Angelique is well again," Aidan told Issie as they sat down for breakfast together. "He's told everyone to go home for the weekend and we've all got next week off as well. Rupert's totally furious because it's costing a fortune to delay filming.

"On the plus side," he added, smiling, "that means you get to go home and see Blaze. I know you've been missing her lots."

"What about Stardust?" Issie said.

Aidan looked down at his plate. He didn't say anything.

"Aidan? What's going on?" Issie felt a chill run up her spine.

"Hester says she's got to go and there's no point in delaying it any longer. There's a horse truck coming for her this afternoon," Aidan said quietly.

"She can't do that!" Issie said.

"Issie…" Aidan began, but Issie didn't stop to listen. She had pushed her breakfast aside and was striding off out of the dining hall.

She found Aunt Hester down at the main arena training Destiny on the lunge rein. Hester saw her niece approaching and called the black stallion to a halt. "Good timing," she said. "I've just finished with him. You can help me put him away."

"Aunty Hess," Issie said as they walked, "Aidan just

told me you're getting rid of Stardust. What's going to happen to her?"

Hester was taken aback. "I was going to tell you before they came for her. I'm going to call her owners today and tell them to come and get her," Hester sighed. "I kept hoping that she'd improve. But she hasn't. And I can't keep a dangerous horse on the set, Issie. I've tried to change her, to understand her, but I can't do it any more. She's beyond my help."

Issie felt her heart quicken as her aunt said this. She suddenly realised there was still hope – she had an idea.

"Aunty Hess! Maybe you and I can't change her, but I think we both know someone who can."

Her aunt looked at her. "What are you talking about, Issie?"

"Tom Avery," Issie said. "Aunty Hess, what if Tom could fix her?"

"Tom? He's an excellent horseman, Isadora, but we simply don't have the time to—"

"Aunty Hess!" Issie objected. "We've got the whole weekend – and all of next week! Rupert has just called off filming until Angelique's foot gets better. That gives us loads of time! Don't phone her owners just yet. Let me take Stardust home to Winterflood Farm until filming starts again. I'll explain it all to Tom and ask him to help us."

Hester looked uncertain.

"Please, Aunty Hess? It's worth a shot," Issie said.

Hester nodded. "All right, Isadora. Tom has helped us out before. He has tricks up his sleeve that even I haven't seen, so maybe he *can* pull it off. You have a week until you're due back on set. Let's see what he comes up with!"

"Thanks, Aunty Hess! I'm going to call him right now!" Issie beamed. Then she turned on her heels and began to run back towards the barracks.

Of course! If anyone could help Stardust, it was Tom Avery. Issie felt her heart soar.

"Tell him he's got his work cut out," Hester called after her. "Stardust had better be a changed horse when she comes back or she's off the film!"

When Avery arrived to pick up Issie, Stella, Kate, Natasha and Stardust that afternoon, Issie was over the moon to see her instructor. The girls had so much to tell Tom, they didn't shut up for the entire drive home. Issie quickly filled Avery in on all the dramas, including Stardust and Angelique.

"She's impossible!" Issie said.

"Who is? Stardust?" Tom replied.

"No – Angelique! Stardust never stood on her foot! It's not my fault, but Rupert thinks I did it! I mean, just because she's a famous film star. And she's always rude to everyone and she has all these assistants racing after her."

"Well, celebrities are used to having people catering to their every whim—" Tom began, but Issie cut him off again.

"I don't know what to do with her. I've tried to work with her, but she ignores me and she's so arrogant. It's like she's a stuck-up girl who thinks she's better than everyone else."

"Who are we talking about now – Angelique?"

"No! Stardust!" Issie said. "I'm talking about Stardust now, Tom – keep up! I mean, I know she's a horse, but honestly she's worse than Angelique. She's like a bratty star or something!"

"Issie, that's it! You've hit the nail on the head," Tom said.

"What?"

"Stardust's been getting the star treatment – well, no more! If we're going to figure out what's making Stardust misbehave then we need to get her listening to us. The first thing we have to do is bring this mare back down to earth!"

Issie's eyes widened. "Tom! You're right. Stardust's been spoilt – and it's impossible to figure out what's wrong when she's being fussed over like a star on a film set!"

"Exactly. What she needs to straighten her out is to be treated like a normal horse again, like she's not anything special at all – like she's just one of the gang."

"How do we do that though?" Issie asked.

Avery smiled. "It's rather obvious when you think about it," he said. "If we want to make her act like a regular horse, we have to send her to a place where regular horses go." He looked at Issie.

"Tomorrow, Stardust is going to pony club."

Chapter 10

"Mum! Have you seen my pony-club jumper?" Issie called out as she ran down the stairs in her jodhpurs and white shirt. She found her mother in the kitchen making breakfast – and her pony-club jersey folded neatly over the back of the kitchen chair.

"It was buried under a huge pile of dirty clothing in your room and I figured you might need it. I washed it for you," Mrs Brown smiled, passing Issie the navy jumper. "Now sit down and eat a proper breakfast, please. No racing off hungry. You've got a big day."

It was 8 a.m. by the time Issie set off for Winterflood Farm on her bike. Pony-club rally didn't start until ten, which left plenty of time to prepare Stardust – and check on Blaze.

Avery stepped out of his front door as Issie parked her bike in the driveway. "Blaze is in the foaling stall," he said.

"Why?" Issie felt her heart race. "Tom… is she…"

"No, no," Avery said. "She's got three weeks to go until she's due to foal, Issie. I'm just getting her used to the stall. I bring her in for an hour or so each day now so that she'll feel comfortable in there when her foal finally arrives."

Issie ran round the side of the stable block to the foaling stall and stuck her head over the door. "Hey, girl," she called softly to her horse. Blaze raised her head from her hay net and nickered back in reply as she walked over to meet Issie.

"Wow!" Issie was shocked by the size of Blaze's tummy. "She's enormous! She's twice the size she was when I left a week ago."

Issie ran her hands over the mare's belly. "How can you tell when the foal is due?"

Her instructor gestured for her to bend down beside him and look between the mare's hind legs. "Look at her udders," he said. "You see how they haven't filled up yet?

At the moment Blaze's udders are full in the morning, but during the day the milk seems to go away again as she moves around. That will change and by the time the foal is due the udders will stay full all the time and you'll see little drops of colostrum, which is like a thick milk, coming out of the teats."

"What will happen when the foal comes out? How will it reach the milk?" Issie asked.

Avery smiled. "Foals aren't like human babies, you know. They're tough customers. Within the first half-hour of foaling, the mother will lick the foal dry and then the newborn will stand up all by itself and take its first drink."

"So the foal doesn't need our help?" Issie asked.

"I didn't say that," Avery said, looking serious. "There's still a lot that can go wrong, and Blaze will need our help to make sure that her foal is delivered safe and sound. That's why we have the foaling monitor." Avery picked up a small black box which he attached to Blaze's halter. "It should set off an alarm and let us know the minute she's in labour. Then we can bring her into the stall where it's safe and dry and warm for her to have her baby."

"Why don't we just keep her in here?" Issie asked.

"Mares get restless," Avery said, opening the stall door and leading Blaze out into the stable courtyard. "They like to move around and graze in the last few weeks. They hate being cooped up in the stall."

He looked at Issie. "Don't worry. I'll bring her in if the weather gets bad or if she's showing signs of foaling." He looked at his watch. "Come on. I'll put Blaze back in her paddock. You'd better catch Stardust and get her float bandages on so we can truck her to the club. It's nearly time to go."

Issie felt her stomach do a somersault as the horse truck turned down the gravel road to the Chevalier Point grounds.

"It feels like forever since I last rode here," she said.

"It has been a while, hasn't it?" agreed Avery, at the driver's wheel in the truck cab next to her. "I now declare winter officially over. The first rally of the season is here."

Chevalier Point Pony Club was bursting with signs of spring. The three pony-club paddocks were all bright green with new grass, dotted with the occasional cluster of snowdrops.

Everywhere you looked the club grounds were buzzing with activity. A long row of floats and trucks was already parked underneath the row of giant magnolia trees in the first paddock, and horses were being unloaded, groomed and saddled up. Riders in pristine white jodhpurs wearing the club colours were dashing in and out of the clubrooms. Meanwhile, in the far paddocks, Issie could see instructors and parents preparing the jumping courses and games for the day.

"Look! Stella and Kate are here already." Issie pointed under the far tree where Toby and Coco were tied up. The girls waved excitedly at Issie as Avery pulled the truck up next to them. As Issie and Avery jumped down out of the truck, Stella ran over to them.

"This is so cool!" she said. "I can't believe you've really brought Stardust to pony club with you!"

Avery gave Stella a stern look. "Stella, I need you to remember that the whole point of bringing Stardust along to pony-club rally day is to make her feel like a regular horse. Which won't happen if you stand around with your mouth hanging open gawping at her, will it?"

"But, Tom!" Stella grumbled. "Wait till everyone finds out that Stardust is really—"

"No, Stella!" Tom snapped. "You mustn't tell anyone that Stardust is really a movie horse. She's not to receive any special treatment or fuss. As far as you're concerned, she's just an ordinary pony-club mount. OK?"

Stella sniffed at this. "Well, Coco *is* just an ordinary pony-club mount and I make a fuss of her all the time!"

Avery sighed. "Stella, you know perfectly well what I mean. And I'm quite serious – this applies to all of you." He looked at the girls sternly.

"I still don't get it," Kate said. "Why did you bring her to the rally anyway?"

Avery went round to the back of the horse truck and began to undo the tail bolts. "Stardust has been treated like a celebrity," he said. "She's been spoilt and it's made her sour and bored. She's desperate for attention and she's willing to behave badly to get it." Avery lowered the ramp. "In the past her bad behaviour got her just what she wanted – more attention! It's become like a game, you see? What we need to do is ignore her when she's naughty and stop fussing over her. It's very important today that everyone should treat Stardust like a normal pony at a normal pony-club rally."

This proved to be easier said than done. Issie was leading Stardust out of the truck when her friends Dan and Ben arrived on their ponies.

"Look! It's the movie stars! Can I have your autograph?" Ben teased as he pulled his bay pony, Max, up alongside Avery's horse truck.

"Hey, I hope you haven't forgotten your friends now that you're all famous," Dan grinned. He was riding Kismit, his elegant, fleabitten grey.

When the two boys saw the graceful palomino, they were stunned. Dan ran his eyes over the mare's long silvery mane and her fine legs with their sparkling white socks. He was clearly impressed. "She's amazing!" he said.

"Is that one of the horses from the film?" Ben asked. "What's her name?"

"This is Stardust," Issie said as she tied the palomino up to Avery's truck. "She plays Seraphine – she's Angelique Adams's horse in the movie. But please, guys, don't make a fuss. No one is supposed to know." She turned to Stella and Kate. "Can you guys explain the whole deal to them? You know, what Avery said about treating her like a normal horse? I need to saddle Stardust up or I'll be late. You go on ahead and I'll meet you there."

As Issie tightened the girth the palomino tried to get in a vicious nip. Issie managed to dodge her the first time, but when the mare tried to nip her a second time, her teeth actually connected and tore a rip in Issie's best pony-club shirt.

"Stardust!" Issie squealed. She examined her arm. Thank goodness the mare had only got the shirt, not her arm!

Horse bites could really, really hurt. Issie took a deep breath. It wasn't just the shock of the bite that had shaken her. It was the disappointment of Stardust's bad behaviour. The other day at the stable she had thought the mare was beginning to like her. But Stardust was as unpredictable and nasty as ever.

Don't let her get to you. Just ignore her bad behaviour, Issie told herself and stuck her foot into the stirrup, bouncing up into the saddle. "C'mon, Little Miss Movie Star!" she muttered as they set off for the arena.

In the dressage arena Avery's class was already under way. Natasha was at the head of the ride, looking snooty on her gorgeous rose-grey gelding, Faberge.

"You're late," Natasha snapped at Issie as she trotted briskly past her. "Just because you're riding a movie star doesn't mean you can be late for the rally, you know."

Natasha was followed around the arena by Stella, Kate, Ben and Dan, Annabel Willets on her palomino gelding Eddie, and the Miller sisters, Pip and Catherine, who rode matching greys.

"Join in at the end of the ride, Issie," Avery called out to her. Issie trotted Stardust into the arena and joined up at the rear of the ride behind Pip Miller and her little grey, Mitzy. Pip turned round and gave Issie a shy smile. "Is this your new pony? She's beautiful," she whispered over her shoulder.

Yeah, beauty – and the beast! Issie thought to herself.

Stardust hadn't even managed to trot once round the arena before she began to act up. She would trot for a few strides and then stop dead and Issie would be jerked forward in the saddle each time.

"What's wrong?" Avery called out to Issie.

"She keeps being nappy. She won't listen to me," Issie said, trying not to sound frustrated. "Every time I ask her to trot she stops dead."

"Here," Avery said, walking over to her. He reached up to hand Issie his brown leather riding whip, which he always carried with him. "Take my whip. You don't have to use it on her, but if she knows you are carrying it, it may help to get her to respect your leg and move forward." Avery stepped forward and held the whip aloft for Issie to take.

"Stand still, Stardust!" Issie said gruffly as the mare tried to back away. "Stop it!" But Stardust wouldn't calm down. The mare was fretting and dancing about the arena, trying to back away from Avery. As he stepped forward again to try and give Issie the whip, the mare suddenly rose up on her hind legs, her hooves flailing wildly in the air.

"Stardust, no!" Issie screamed, grabbing on to the mare's neck with both hands. Then, as Stardust dropped back down to the ground, Issie instinctively knew what was coming next. She'd been here before. Quickly, she leapt out of the saddle and stood beside Stardust.

"Tom! It's just like that time in the arena on the film set," Issie shouted. "I think she's going to roll!" Issie was right. Stardust had dropped to her knees now and was about to lie down – and she was wearing Issie's favourite saddle! It was her Bates Maestro – the dressage saddle that Avery had given her. If Stardust rolled on it, she would break the tree and the saddle would be ruined!

"Hold her by the bridle. Don't let her roll!" Avery shouted. He rushed forward, still holding the riding crop and waved his arms at Stardust. "Get up!" he shouted at her.

Stardust seemed so spooked by this that instead of lying down to roll, she promptly leapt back up to her feet again and backed away from Avery, snorting and pawing the ground.

"Is she crazy or something?" Natasha said as she sat on Faberge and watched the whole commotion.

"Uh-uh," Avery said. "Quite the opposite. Stardust's a very bright horse and she's been trained to behave like this." He dropped the riding crop that he was still holding in his right hand and walked towards the trembling palomino.

"It's OK, Stardust," Avery said gently. "It's OK." This time the mare didn't back away as he took hold of the reins and led her out of the arena with Issie running at his side.

"You were right, Issie," Avery said as they walked Stardust back towards the horse trucks. "When you said that maybe something you had done had given Stardust her cue to rear and roll like that? You were dead right."

He turned to Issie. "When you were training in the arena that day and she reared and tried to roll on you, were you carrying a whip?"

Issie shook her head. "No, I wasn't," she said. Then she remembered. "But I was carrying a sword! A broadsword. I had just pulled one out of the props bin when Stardust started acting up!" Issie's mind began to race. "And the props guy, he handed me a sword too, just before Stardust bolted that day when we were filming the chase scene."

Avery nodded. "Issie, I think we've figured out what's wrong with Stardust. Hester was right. Those trainers on her last film must have done this."

"Done what?" Issie felt her heart sink – she knew what Avery was going to say.

"Issie, they beat her. With sticks and whips. They must have been trying to train her to do a trick – probably a trick where she needed to rear and roll – and they lost their temper and hit her hard. Look here! There's a freshly healed scar on her near shoulder. That must be from where the whip struck her."

Avery shook his head. "The wound has healed, but horses never forget. Now Stardust is terrified whenever she sees a whip, or a broadsword – any big stick. You were carrying a sword both times when she misbehaved on the film set. That's what set her off. In fact, I'd bet you that all of Stardust's bad behaviour, even the biting and the bad temper, began after they started to hit her. She's not really nasty, she's just acting in self-defence out of fear. She's scared of being hit again."

"Poor Stardust! How terrible!" Issie groaned.

"No," Avery said firmly. "This is good."

"Good?" Issie boggled at Avery.

Avery shook his head. "Don't you see, Issie? Now that we know what's worrying Stardust, that's half the battle won."

"But, Tom," Issie protested, "Stardust is a stunt

horse. If she can't be ridden with a sword then she'll still be kicked off the movie!"

Avery looked at the palomino. "Well then, we'll just have to retrain her, won't we? By this time next week, Stardust must be ready to rejoin the Daredevil Ponies – and we're going to make sure that she is."

Chapter 11

With hardly any time, every day was crucial in Stardust's retraining programme. The morning after the disastrous pony-club rally, Issie arrived at Winterflood Farm at seven a.m. and found Tom waiting for her in the kitchen with bacon, eggs and toast.

"This will be our routine for the next week," he said, dishing up grilled mushrooms on to her plate. "We'll be doing long days training. You need a good breakfast to get you started."

"Thanks," Issie nodded and asked nervously, "Tom? What is it exactly that we're going to do today?"

"Do you remember the desensitisation obstacle course that Hester put you through?" Avery asked.

"Uh-huh," Issie said. "Stardust was just fine about

everything – the blankets and the lights and that stuff, but she went crazy as soon as I tried to pick up a sword."

Avery nodded. "For a normal stunt horse a desensitisation course will solve any problems like that and make a horse bombproof – but Stardust isn't a normal horse. She's super-smart and she's been hurt, badly beaten, so she's got a very good reason to be scared of sticks, swords, whips – anything that she can be hit with."

"So how do we get rid of her fear?" Issie said.

"Same technique but more focused," Avery said, "for which we will need these…" He pulled a big leather bag out from beneath the kitchen table. It contained a broadsword, a riding crop, a big branch and a stock whip.

"…and also lots of these!" Avery pulled out another bag, which was full to the brim with fresh carrots.

"I'm not sure I get it." Issie was confused.

"Don't worry, it will all become clear," Avery said, grabbing a halter off the kitchen bench. "I'm going to go and catch Stardust while you finish up your brekkie. I'll meet you at the stables. It's time to get to work."

For the first stage of desensitisation, Avery put Stardust in a loose box. "She needs to be free to move around, but she mustn't be able to get too far away from you," he explained to Issie.

"We'll leave her loose in her halter without a lead rope. Don't tie her up," Avery instructed. "She needs to be able to back away if she wants to. You want her to feel comfortable." He passed Issie the bag of whips, swords and sticks. "We're going to get her used to these. I want you to go into her stall and rub them all over her body."

"But she's terrified of them…" Issie began to protest.

"Exactly," Avery said. "She needs to learn that a whip or a sword will not do her any harm as long as you are around. Slowly but firmly I want you to pick up the various sticks and use them like grooming brushes – walk around her and touch her firmly but gently with them. Stroke her with them as if they were an extension of your own hands. She's going to be nervous at first. Very nervous probably. Let her move away from you if she wants. Take it slowly. Then, when she's accepting your touch, give her a carrot because she's been good. After a while, she'll learn to associate being touched with the whips and swords with good feelings instead of bad – that's what the carrots are for."

Issie thought that Avery's plan made total sense – until she got into the stall with Stardust. The minute she took the first broadsword out of the bag, Stardust backed away from her, completely terrified, and cowered in the corner of the stall.

"Tom?" Issie said. "What now?" She didn't see how she could possibly rub the sword over Stardust's body when the mare wouldn't even let her get near.

"Keep the sword lowered and don't go to her," Avery advised calmly. "Sit down in the middle of the stall with your sword and your carrot and let her come to you."

And so Issie sat and waited. And waited. They only had one week to retrain Stardust and here she was, wasting time by sitting in a stall doing nothing!

"Stay there and don't move," Avery insisted.

Almost an hour later, just as Issie felt her patience completely ebbing away, the curious and hungry Stardust could stand it no longer. The palomino finally summoned up the courage to step forward. She took three tentative steps and then craned her neck, nuzzling the carrot out of Issie's hand.

"Good girl!" Issie said, letting Stardust eat the carrot which she held in her lap next to the sword. "Good girl!"

After that, Issie spent the rest of the morning slowly

coaxing Stardust to stand still in her stall while Issie fed her carrots with one hand, while stroking her with the sword in her other hand. By lunchtime, the mare would stand without flinching as Issie gently ran the sword over her neck and shoulders.

Issie wasn't at all happy with her progress. "It's not fast enough. We'll never have her ready at this rate!" she grumbled to Tom when she left Stardust in her stall and came inside for lunch.

"Nonsense!" Avery said sharply. "You've made huge strides today. You just don't know it yet. Remember, this is a horse that hates whips and swords more than anything and you had her eating a carrot while you stroked her with a broadsword! Trust me, this is big stuff, Issie. By the time you get in that stall tomorrow, she'll be a changed horse. Mark my words."

Avery was right. By the next morning, Stardust was letting Issie run the wooden broadsword all over her body, even under her belly and down her legs.

"I don't believe it!" Issie said. "Yesterday she was so strung out, I couldn't get near her."

"Once you build trust, anything is possible," Avery said. "She's getting more faith in you all the time, Issie."

It was true. Stardust seemed almost pleased to see Issie

now when she arrived each morning to lead her in from her paddock for her training session.

Issie's daily routine revolved entirely around rehabilitating the palomino. In the morning she would work in the loose box with the swords and the whips. Then in the afternoon she would put Stardust back in her paddock and Stella or Kate would come over and the girls would stage mock swordfights with each other right under Stardust's nose.

"She needs to get comfortable with the idea of the swords being banged about right next to her and know that they're not going to hurt her," Avery explained.

Each time Stardust stood still and didn't spook during their swordplay, Issie would pause to feed the mare a carrot and give her a pat before starting a fresh battle with Kate or Stella.

While they were doing this, Avery would walk around the paddock, sticking swords into the ground in odd places. There were even swords poking out of the ground next to Stardust's water trough and feed bin. "If she becomes familiar with them and knows they won't hurt her then there's no reason for her to be afraid any more," Tom replied when Issie asked him what he was doing.

After the mock swordfights each day, Issie would

saddle up Stardust for the final phase of her training, which Avery referred to as a "spoilt brat reality check". "Stardust has been stuck on film sets for so long. It will do her good to have a look at the real world and live like a regular horse for once!" Avery pointed out.

So Issie would saddle up and hack her out from Winterflood Farm to the River Paddock to meet up with Stella and Kate. As Stardust began to settle in and enjoy her outings with Toby and Coco, they would canter along the river bank and Issie would pretend it was a cross-country tournament and ride Stardust over fallen logs or ditches that they came across along the way. It turned out the mare loved to jump and would always pick up her feet nicely over a fence, never hesitating or baulking.

As each day went by, the palomino's newfound confidence in her rider showed. By the end of the week Issie could canter her along the grass riverbank between Winterflood Farm and the River Paddock on a loose rein without any fear of the horse bolting. On Friday, when Issie mounted up in the paddock and Avery passed her a sword, Stardust stood perfectly still and didn't flinch. By Saturday, Issie could sit on Stardust's back and swing her sword above her head without the mare batting an eyelid. And on Sunday, when they went back to pony club for the next rally day, Stardust didn't even seem to notice that Issie was riding her the whole time with a whip in her hand.

As she rode into the arena, with Stardust trotting along neatly, her neck arched and her ears pricked forward, Issie felt like they were ready for anything. But there was one obstacle she hadn't counted on.

"Isn't that sweet?" Natasha Tucker said as she saw Issie approaching. "Taking her for one last outing before she heads off to the glue factory."

"Very funny, Natasha," Issie sighed, "but for your information, Stardust is totally retrained and ready to go back to work."

Natasha pulled a face. "Are you planning on bolting again and ruining another day's shooting?"

"That wasn't Stardust's fault," Issie said, standing up for her horse.

"I didn't say it was her fault," Natasha smirked. "A good stunt rider would have stopped her. That's why Rupert should have picked me!"

Unfortunately it was games practice at pony club that morning and just when Issie thought she'd seen the last of Natasha, she found herself stuck with her again. The snooty blonde was racing against Issie in the bending race. Issie knew Natasha didn't really mean to be so horrible and it must be awful for her right now with her parents splitting up and everything. Still, she really could be a total cow! Issie couldn't help but feel a glow of satisfaction when Stardust aced the bending race and beat Natasha and Faberge by a whole two poles.

Things got even better after games practice. Avery had set up a jumping course and Stardust went totally clear on her first round, taking decent-sized fences with ease.

"Stardust is, like, a total pony-club superstar!" Stella said, shaking her head in amazement.

The biggest shock, though, came at lunchtime. Issie was untacking the mare when suddenly Stardust swung her head around. Issie panicked, thinking she was trying to bite her again. But instead of trying to nip, Stardust gave a friendly nicker. Then she reached over and nuzzled Issie gently on the arm.

"Oh, you're saying hello!" Issie giggled. "Well, hey there, girl! You startled me." She couldn't believe it. Something had changed in Stardust. The steely aggression was gone from her eyes. It turned out she loved being a regular pony-club horse!

It had been a great week, Issie decided. Her plan to bring Stardust home had really worked. The mare had improved so much each day. Not only that, the week at home had given Issie a chance to be with Blaze.

Every evening, after Issie had finished Stardust's training, she would take both her horses their hard feed. Then she would stay and watch as Blaze ate, talking softly to her mare and marvelling at how enormous her belly was.

Now that Blaze was so close to foaling, Avery had moved the mare into the sheltered paddock closest to the stables. One sunny evening, as Issie leant over the rails of the paddock watching the mare devour her bucket of hard feed, she heard Avery's voice behind her. "Filly or colt?"

"What do you mean?" Issie was confused.

"I mean Blaze's foal. What do you think it will be? A filly or a colt? What are you hoping for?"

"I don't know," Issie said, shaking her head. "I guess I really don't mind. Maybe a filly because then she'd look just like Blaze. She's so beautiful, isn't she, Tom?"

Blaze seemed to be enjoying all the adoration. She looked up from her feed bucket and seemed to shake her head up and down in agreement over her own beauty.

Issie smiled at the mare and then her face turned serious. "Tom, I don't think I can go back to the film set again. I can't leave Blaze behind. What if she starts to foal? I should stay here. She needs me."

"You heard what the vet said when he came out on

Wednesday," Tom replied. "It will be another three weeks at least. By the time Blaze is foaling, the film will be wrapped up and you'll be home again."

"I hope so, Tom," Issie said. "Blaze's foal is going to be special. I can feel it. I want to be there more than anything in the world."

Chapter 12

Hester was waiting anxiously with Aidan when Issie, Avery and the girls returned to the film set on Monday morning.

"Well?" Hester asked nervously as Issie clambered out of the truck cab. "What news? Have you reformed my star? Or do I need to saddle up Athena and tell Rupert the bad news?"

"Come and see for yourself," Issie grinned.

As Avery led Stardust down the truck ramp, Issie grabbed her riding helmet out of the truck. Before anyone could stop her, she had grabbed Stardust by the halter and vaulted lightly on to her bare back.

Issie clucked softly to the mare and steered her with the lead rope in one hand like a cowgirl. She gave Stardust a light tap with her legs and asked the mare to trot. Stardust responded immediately, prancing forward in a light, bouncy trot, circling around the grassy field outside the stables where the horse truck had pulled up.

"Meet the new improved Stardust!" Stella said to Hester as she and Kate joined her and Aidan to watch.

"New and improved?" Hester said. "She's like a totally different horse!"

Stardust had her ears pricked forward and Issie had a huge grin on her face as she urged Stardust on into a gallop and raced her in a loop around the field before pulling up to a sudden halt, spinning round on her hindquarters and cantering back towards Hester, Avery and the others. This time, when she came to a halt in front of the group, Issie tapped her toe lightly against the back of Stardust's right leg. Stardust dropped immediately down on to one knee and lowered her head in a circus bow. Then, as Stardust stood up on all four legs again, Issie vaulted off and ran over to her aunt.

"Well done!" Hester was overjoyed. She grabbed Issie in a huge hug and squeezed her so tight Issie thought she would stop breathing. "You are most definitely my absolutely, all-time favourite niece!"

"I taught her to bow," Issie grinned. "It's the same trick Blaze used to do when she was in the El Caballo Danza

Magnifico You were right, Aunty Hess – she learns tricks really easily. It only took me a day to teach her."

Hester shook her head. "She's a changed horse."

"That was Tom," Issie said. "He figured it out, Aunty Hess. You remember that first day when I rode her in the arena, when Stardust went completely bonkers? It was because she is scared of swords! Her trainers on the last movie must have hit her and she kept thinking that we would hit her too!"

Issie gave the mare a loving pat on her velvet muzzle. "Poor Stardust!" she said. "No wonder she'd turned sour."

"How did you retrain her?" Hester asked.

"We took her to Pony Club." Avery smiled and gave Stardust a firm pat on her glossy palomino neck. "Stardust got a taste of normal horsy life. It was just what she needed to bring her back down to earth again."

"Plus," Issie said, "we spent, like, hours and hours desensitising her so that she's not scared of whips and swords any more. Look! Watch this!" Issie nodded to Avery who picked up a broadsword out of the truck and threw it to her.

The sword sailed through the air and Issie caught it expertly. Stardust didn't move a muscle as Issie brandished the sword, waving it over her head before slipping it into the sword sheath at her hip.

"Brilliant!" Hester said as she watched her. Then she turned to Avery. "But how do I stop her from playing up again now she's back on the set?"

Avery smiled. "Don't train her," he said.

"What?"

"Just what I said. Stardust has been in dozens of movies – maybe too many for her own good. She knows all the tricks already and she's so used to swords and whips now – you'll have no problems with her any more. Just don't train her – that's my advice. If you spend too much time rehearsing in the arena, there's always the risk she'll start to play up again."

"So what do you suggest instead?" Hester arched a brow at him.

Avery smiled. "Let Issie ride her, Hester. But not in the arena – out there." Avery stared out at the farmland around them. "Let Stardust be a horse again. Give her and Issie the time and space to go wild together. Let them bond with each other."

Hester nodded at this. "Tom, I have a feeling I owe you big time for this one."

"Not at all," Avery smiled. "It was Issie who thought

of it really. She made me realise that sour, bratty movie stars and sour, bratty horses really aren't that different."

"Well then," Hester said, "maybe you can help us with our other little problem?"

"What's that?"

"It's Angelique Adams," Hester said. "She's locked herself in her trailer. She won't come out and she won't speak to anyone – not even Rupert."

"Angelique is throwing a tantrum!" Issie groaned as she threw herself down on one of the big sofas in the palomino barracks. "This is so crazy. We finally sort out Stardust's problems and now Angelique is being a total pain again!"

"Maybe this movie *is* cursed after all!" Kate groaned.

"Ohhh!" Stella squealed. "That's what I said and you all laughed at me!"

"Oh, don't be ridiculous, Stella!" Kate snapped. "I didn't mean it."

"Oh, really?" Stella sniffed. "Well, how do you explain Angelique's behaviour then?"

"Angelique is just a drama queen," Kate said. "You know

she doesn't want to do this movie, but we still haven't figured out why…"

"She won't even come out of her trailer or talk to anyone," Aidan said. "The only person she's letting in to see her is her make-up artist, her assistant and that guy Eugene – the one who's doing the documentary."

"What's going to happen?" Issie asked.

"There's a rumour going around that Rupert is fed up with her," Aidan said. "They say he wants to replace Angelique with some other up-and-coming new Hollywood actress, you know, Nevada Roberts? They say she was Rupert's first choice for the movie anyway and now he wishes he'd never given Angelique the role.

"That's it!" Stella said. "Maybe Angelique is trying to get herself kicked off this movie. We all heard her say that she doesn't want to do it. And now she's getting her wish."

Issie shook her head. "I don't think so. If Angelique gets kicked off the film, it will be so bad for her reputation. I don't see why she keeps embarrassing herself like this. There must be something more to it. Maybe Rupert wants to get rid of her and he's making her look bad?" Issie turned to Aidan. "You said he wants Nevada Roberts instead?"

Aidan nodded. "It makes sense. He probably does want to get rid of her."

"Get rid of who?"

The girls and Aidan turned round to see Natasha standing in the doorway. She must have just been dropped off by her mum because she was holding her bags and looking miserable.

"Hi, Natasha," Issie said. "Ummm, no one. Honest. It was nothing."

"Is someone trying to get rid of me?" Natasha looked at them all darkly. "Well, it wouldn't be the first time today," she said. Then she stormed past everyone. "I should have known you'd all be backstabbing me again!"

"But, Natasha, we really weren't..." Issie started.

"Oh, leave her, Issie!" Stella said. "We've got bigger problems to worry about without bothering with Natasha..."

By that afternoon, though, their problems were over. "Angelique has been talking to Rupert and everything is back on again," Aidan reported to the others. "Rupert has told the crew that we'll shoot tonight instead and do the castle chase scene. He's getting everything ready for it. Hopefully Angelique will have pulled herself together by then and be ready to ride."

"What do you mean we're shooting tonight?" Issie said.

"We're doing that scene, you know, where the vampire riders chase Seraphine and Galatea up the citadel to the black castle?" Aidan explained. "Angelique is supposed to ride it herself. Hester said to tell you to get Stardust ready for her to ride."

Issie had a sick feeling in her tummy that evening as she saddled up Stardust. The mare seemed to sense Issie's nerves and began to shift restlessly in her stall as Issie put on her saddle and bridle.

"Hey there. It's OK, girl," Issie cooed as she adjusted the mare's jewelled noseband. She knew her nerves were making Stardust anxious, but she couldn't help it. "There's nothing wrong. I'm just being silly, that's all," she told the palomino. "At least we're finally friends now, huh, girl?"

Issie had spent two whole hours grooming Stardust this afternoon so that she'd look her best for her big scene. The mare's golden palomino coat glistened and her mane, which was long and silvery white, seemed almost ghostly under the glare of the single bulb in her stable.

Issie ran her stirrups up the leathers and then led the mare out into the stable yard. She mounted up on the mounting block just as Hester came running over towards her. "They're ready for you now on the set," she said.

"Where's Angelique?"

Hester shook her head. "No one knows. She's gone missing. Rupert is looking for her. He's insisting that she has to ride this scene – but if we can't find her then, well, it's going to have to be you."

Hester switched on a torch so that the pair of them could see the track in front of them. Grass track ran between the stables to the film crew trucks and over to the base of the castle mountain. It was lit all the way along with hurricane lamps so that the crew could see where they were going in the dark. It was hard to tell in the gloom, but Issie guessed it was about a kilometre from the stables to the silver crew trucks and then another kilometre again down to the foot of the black mountain.

"Follow me," Hester said, "they're all waiting for you."

She wasn't kidding. When Issie reached the foot of the black mountain there must have been at least thirty crew members bustling about on the set. Lighting crew were setting up enormous scaffolding that ran out of sight down the terraces. The costume department people were running around with armfuls of black capes and the set designers were busily putting the finishing touches on the black castle. One of the crew was painting a strange liquid that looked like snail slime all over the black rocks surrounding the terraces that wound up the mountain.

Issie tied Stardust to one of the silver crew trucks and gazed up at the castle mountain ahead of her. A chill ran down her spine. Angelique hadn't turned up – she would have to ride. She would have to take the terraces at a flat-out gallop with the black horsemen behind her, and then turn to face the hooded vampire riders as their leader, Francis, tried to sink his fangs into Seraphine and suck out the mare's golden palomino blood so that she too became a black, soulless beast…

"Hi there!"

Issie just about jumped out of her skin as she caught a glimpse of a ghoulish white face looming towards her in the black night. She let out a high-pitched squeak.

"Whoaa! You're a bit jumpy tonight, aren't you?" It was Aidan and he was already dressed in his vampire rider costume.

"Yeah," Issie agreed, "I guess I am. It's scary shooting at night, don't you think?"

"Don't worry," Aidan reassured her, "it's perfectly safe. The crew have got all the lighting set up so you can see where you're going. You won't get lost in the dark and ride off the edge of the mountain or anything." His white vampire fangs shone in the light. "It looks like you'll be riding at this rate. I see Angelique hasn't turned up – as usual. What a drama queen! I heard one of the crew say that Angelique's totally living up to her reputation around Hollywood for being a brat. They're saying that Rupert has already approached Nevada Roberts and if Angelique drops out for any reason, Nevada will definitely take her place."

Voices could be heard coming through the darkness towards them. In the half-light of the hurricane lamps Issie recognised Tony, Angelique's personal make-up artist. He was waving a lip gloss in the air and bickering with another man who was also holding make-up brushes. "You've put too much blusher on her!" he was shouting. "She looks vermilion! I am her personal make-up artist – I should be in charge!"

Behind the bickering make-up artists came the rest of Angelique's entourage. There was her assistant carrying the coffee as usual, followed by two women, wearing headsets and carrying clipboards, who were busily ordering other crew members about. Finally, behind them, flanked by two bodyguards, was Angelique Adams.

"Angelique! Angel! Baby! That's it! Look at me! Now just act natural…" Eugene Sneadly was running around them all in circles, his camera lens trained on Angelique. Bob was trailing along behind him. "Great, baby! We're getting amazing footage here!"

Angelique, however, didn't look like she cared about Eugene's amazing footage. Her face was as white as a sheet and she looked completely petrified as she approached the set. As the make-up artist with the blusher brush darted in to fix her make-up again she swatted him away angrily.

"Angelique!" Rupert said, rushing towards her with his own entourage trailing behind him. Rupert embraced his star with a brisk air kiss. "Great to see you! You're looking fantastic! Are you ready to go then? Do you want to mount up and we'll get started? We've got everything in place waiting for you." He turned to his assistant. "Are the vampire horsemen ready to go?"

The assistant nodded. "We've got everyone on set, Rupert. They're waiting on your cue."

"Good, good!" Rupert rubbed his hands together. "Right! Time is money, as they say. So let's get cracking then, shall we?" He smiled at Angelique. The superstar returned his grin with a tense, tight-lipped smile.

"Ummm, the thing is, Rupert, maybe y'all should do this scene without me," Angelique muttered. "I tried to tell that doctor – my foot is still sore and…"

Rupert cut his star off with a glare. "Angelique, I have already delayed filming for a whole week for you. Do you know how much that has cost this production? I've had three different doctors look at your foot and they all say the same thing. You are fine."

Rupert leant forward and lowered his voice to a hiss so that only Angelique could hear. "Now, you spoilt brat, you listen to me. You have a contract with this film company. We can't keep making this movie without you. You are going to get on this horse right now and you are going to ride. Or you can quit right here and now and I will replace you with Nevada Roberts. I know you must have heard the rumour and I can tell you that it's quite true. I won't have you ruining my movie. So why don't you just grow up and get on the horse."

"The thing is—" Angelique began, but she was interrupted by Eugene.

"Angelique, baby!" he boomed. "Rupert is right. You have to do this scene." He grabbed the starlet by the elbow and pulled her roughly away from the crowd. "Honey, we need you to get in the picture! Here I am making a behind-the-scenes documentary and so far I have nothing!"

"But I—" Angelique tried to speak again but Eugene cut her off.

"Baby! This is an Angelique Adams movie, right? And who are you? You're Angelique Adams! You have to do this, sweetheart! This is your movie." Eugene flung his arms out. "All these people here are waiting just for you. This is your moment, baby! Now get on that horse over there and show them how it's done."

Angelique took a deep breath and then she turned to Issie. "You heard the man," she snipped. "Get off my horse. This is my movie and I'm riding this scene!"

"Way to go, Angel baby!" Eugene egged her on as he hoisted the video camera on to his shoulder again and began filming. He looked around him frantically. "Bob? Where the hell are you? Get over here, Bob! Now! I need sound!" Bob, who had been loitering at the back of the entourage, raced forward with his sound boom as Angelique marched right up to Issie and stood with her hands on her hips.

"Are you deaf or something?" Angelique pouted. "I told you to get off my horse."

Issie reluctantly dismounted from Stardust's back and handed Angelique the reins. Angelique reached out her hand to take them as if she were reaching out to touch an electric fence. It looked like she thought the reins were going to bite her. Then she turned to Issie again.

"Help me get up on him," she ordered.

"Her," Issie said.

"What?"

"Stardust isn't a 'him', she's a 'her'," Issie said.

"Oh, what-ever!" Angelique said, trying to sound tough. But Issie noticed there was a tremor in the starlet's voice as she spoke.

"Anyway," Angelique continued, "I said help me up."

Issie stood next to Stardust and cupped her hands so that Angelique could put her knee in Issie's palms for a leg-up. But the starlet just looked at her blankly. "What are you doing?" she growled.

"I'm giving you a leg-up," Issie said. "Put your knee in my hands and I'll push you up."

Angelique sniffed. "I knew that!" she said. "I know all about horses!" She put her knee in Issie's hands, but rather than bouncing up like riders naturally do,

Angelique sagged like a sack of potatoes. Issie found herself heaving her up like she was tossing a caber to throw her into the saddle. Angelique came down with a crash and Stardust lurched forward with shock.

As Stardust moved beneath her, Angelique squealed and made a frantic grab for the front of the saddle with both hands as if she were in danger and desperate to hang on. Issie instinctively grabbed the reins and held Stardust steady until Angelique picked the reins up. Issie couldn't help noticing that the actress held them in her clenched fists like a toddler gripping the steering wheel of a toy car.

"Where are the thingummys?" Angelique asked Issie as she looked down at her feet. Then she saw the stirrup irons dangling by her ankles. "Oh, there they are!" She shoved her feet into the stirrups then began flapping her arms and wiggling her feet around. It was like she was doing the chicken dance.

"Well!" she said to Issie. "Why won't she go?" Angelique gave Stardust a poke in the neck with her finger. "Come on then, horsy. What are you waiting for? Gee-up!"

And in that instant Issie realised the truth. The shock made her blood run cold. She had discovered Angelique's secret. There was no way that anyone who had ever ridden a horse before would hold the reins like that. Or flap their arms to make a horse go. *Ohmygod*, Issie thought, *it all makes sense*. The fake broken foot, the temper tantrums in her trailer, the way Angelique always made sure she wasn't standing too close to the horses. Even the fights with her agent and pretending she was injured so that Rupert had to stop filming for a week. Issie saw it all now. Of course! It was so obvious. And so awful! Angelique Adams, the star of The *Palomino Princess*, had a secret all right. She couldn't ride!

Chapter 13

Angelique flapped her arms wildly, jerking at Stardust's mouth. As Issie watched the mare getting more and more upset. She couldn't help herself; she rushed forward and made a lunge at Stardust's reins. "Stop it! You're going to spook her!" Issie shouted.

Angelique glared down at her. "Don't you dare tell me what to do!" she sneered at Issie. "I'm the star of this movie – nobody tells me what to do."

Issie didn't know what to say. Angelique was right. She was the star and Issie was a total nobody – a lowly stunt rider.

"Listen," Issie hissed under her breath, "Angelique, I know the truth. I know that you can't ride – it's OK, honest, I won't tell anyone. But please, trust me. You can't ride Stardust in this scene. She's a highly-strung, temperamental mare – she's not a beginner's pony. It's not safe. You'll hurt yourself. Please, let me ride her instead. I'll make an excuse for you. I'll tell Rupert that you've hurt your foot again or something. Please?"

Angelique fixed Issie with a cold stare. "I don't know what you're talking about!" she snapped. "I am a great rider. And I'm the star of this movie – you're not going to replace me. Now back off and leave me alone!"

"But…"

"You heard her. Back off – now!" A gruff voice behind Issie made her jump. She turned round to see Eugene looking menacingly at her.

"Eugene, please. Angelique can't—" Issie was cut off by Eugene who hissed at her in a low whisper.

"You think I don't know what's going on? I know exactly what's going on here, kid! You stay out of it and leave Angelique to me." Eugene turned to the trembling superstar and gave a broad grin.

"Angel baby, I'm telling you, you'll be fine. Don't listen to the kid here. Remember you're the star, baby! Look at you! You are a great rider – a natural! Now get out there and break a leg!"

Issie was shocked. "What?" Eugene shrugged. "That's

what we say in Hollywood – break a leg. It means good luck. You got a problem with that, kid? Now why don't you shut your trap before I shut it for you?"

"Hey, hey… what on earth is going on over here?" Issie saw Rupert striding over towards them. "Angelique? Eugene?" Rupert looked concerned. "Do we have some kind of problem here?"

"Rupert, baby!" Eugene's greasy charm went into overdrive at the arrival of the director. "Rupert, things are great! No problems at all. Angel was just giving this sweet little stunt rider here a few pointers on how to ride a horse. She's totally ready to go, aren't you, Angel?"

Angelique looked at Eugene. Then she gave Rupert a reluctant, forced smile. "Sure, Rupert. I'm ready."

"Excellent!" Rupert said. "If you'll head down to the marker at the foot of the hill where the vampire riders are gathered, please? Can we have lighting technicians ready on the set too? We need to have the lights shining on the terraces as the horses ride up the mountain. We'll do this first take with the crew set up at long distance and then we'll move in for the close-ups later."

Eugene elbowed his way past Issie and grabbed Stardust by the reins. "Beat it, kid," he growled at Issie. "I'll take it from here."

Angelique flapped her legs uselessly against Stardust's sides. "I still can't make him go, Eugene! Can you lead me?"

"I've already told you," Issie said through gritted teeth, "Stardust is a her, not a him, and you need to stop kicking her! She's sensitive."

"Hey, kid!" Eugene barked. "Are you deaf? Get out of here!" He took Stardust's reins and began to lead the mare over to where the vampire riders were standing, waiting to start shooting.

"Bob?" Eugene looked around behind him. "Bob! Get over here now! We're gonna get Angelique's big scene on film for the documentary! We don't want to miss this. Come on – let's hustle!"

Issie watched helplessly as Eugene led Stardust down to the foot of the mountain terraces with Bob trailing behind. She could feel her heart racing. Eugene was crazy! Didn't he realise that Angelique could get killed if she tried to ride a dangerous stunt like this? Issie didn't care what he said, she had to try and stop this. She needed help.

Aunty Hess! Her aunt was her best hope. She had to find her and explain everything. Rupert would have to listen to Hester. After all, she was his head trainer.

She looked about her frantically. Aunty Hess was

probably still at the trucks with the rest of the film crew, back up the track at least a kilometre away from the black castle. If Issie was going to get to her aunt in time, she would have to run.

She set off as fast as she could along the grassy track towards the trucks. Although the track was lit with hurricane lamps, it was still pretty dark in places, too dark to see where she was putting her feet. The grass on the track was thick and slippery with dew, which didn't help either, and she had to keep ducking past various runners and assistants who were all hurrying in the other direction, getting ready for shooting to begin. At one point, she nearly lost her footing, slipping over on the track and almost sliding down the steep bank to the ditch below.

By the time Issie finally reached the silver trucks, she was wet, muddy and exhausted.

"Ohmygod!" Stella said when she saw her. "What are you doing back here? I thought you were down on the set with Stardust and Angelique? What's wrong?"

Issie fought to get her breath back, sucking in great gulps of air. "No… time… to… explain… Must… find… Aunty Hess."

"But, Issie," Kate said, "Hester's not here. One of the

black horses threw a shoe and she's gone back to the stables to find the farrier."

Issie felt her heart sink. The stables were another kilometre at least from here. She would never make it. She was too tired to run that far. Besides, by the time she reached Hester, they would already have started filming and it would be too late.

"Issie," Stella said, "what is it? You have to tell us what's wrong."

Issie was still puffed. She took another deep breath and then managed to get the words out. "It's Angelique," she said. "She can't ride."

"What do you mean?" Stella said. "Of course Angelique can ride. She's a great rider. We heard her say so herself."

Issie nodded. "Yeah, but we've never actually seen her ride, have we? Until tonight. I just watched her get on to Stardust. She doesn't have a clue what she's doing. I'm pretty sure she's never even been on a horse before. In fact, I'd say she's terrified of them!"

"But, Issie!" Kate said. "If she can't ride, where is she now?"

"She's on Stardust! I told her not to ride. I told her I'd stunt-double for her, but Angelique said she was the star and then Eugene told me to beat it and…" Issie trailed off. "She wouldn't listen. She's going to ride the scene herself. She's going to get herself killed."

"We have to tell Hester," Kate agreed. "She can stop this."

Stella nodded. "Kate and I will go. Issie, you go back down the track and try and stall them until we get there."

Issie agreed. "Tell Aunty Hess she has to hurry. They're about to start shooting really soon. They were just getting the vampire horsemen sorted when I left. It can't be long now before they begin."

As Kate and Stella ran off together towards the stables, Issie bent over to catch her breath. She was exhausted. And what was the point in running all the way back again? Angelique and Rupert wouldn't listen to her.

She bent down, put her hands on her knees and took a deep breath. Even if she didn't care what happened to the spoilt brat movie star, she had to get back and try and help Stardust. If Angelique fell off, then Rupert was bound to blame the palomino and all of Issie's hard work rehabilitating the mare would be worthless.

Issie stood up and began to head back towards the path. Whether Rupert believed her or not, she decided she had to try.

There was no one else on the track now – all the crew were already down on the set, standing by, waiting for filming to begin. She was all alone, the hurricane lamps casting spooky shadows over the narrow grassy path in front of her as she ran. At certain points along the track the lamps had gone out completely. The moon had gone behind the clouds as well, so at times the path ahead was pitch-black. Issie could barely see where she was going.

Suddenly she let out a squeal as she felt the ground falling away beneath her feet. In the dark she had veered completely off the track and now she was sliding down the slippery grass bank, unable to regain her footing as she fell. As she plummeted, she reached out her hands, grabbing at the grass to stop herself and felt the vicious sting of blackberry prickles piercing her skin. Unable to hang on, Issie curled into a ball instead, with her hands over her head as she slid down the steep slope.

When she reached the bottom of the bank she hit the dirt with a thud. The fall had made her woozy and it took her a few seconds to stand up. Carefully, so as not to stick her hands into any more prickles, Issie gingerly pushed herself up off the ground and looked around. Above her, she could just about make out the track, lit by the dotted line of the hurricane lamps.

Behind her was pitch-blackness. The only way out was back up the steep blackberry bank.

This proved to be easier said than done. The grass was slippery and every time Issie found herself gaining some ground, she would mistakenly grab a hunk of blackberry vine and squeal in pain as the vicious prickles dug into her hands. She kept crawling on her hands and knees until she had got through the worst of it and was almost at the top – the steepest bit. Issie felt her heart sink as she tried to climb over the edge and found herself slipping back. It was impossible to get back up again! She clawed at the mud and grass, dragging herself towards the edge, before sliding back down once more.

I can't do it, Issie thought. *I can't get up. I'm too tired.* She clung on for a moment, her hands grasping the wet grass, her belly pressed against the mud, and felt hot tears welling in her eyes.

Then suddenly Issie found herself plunged into complete darkness as the hurricane lamp on the path ahead of her seemed to disappear. She strained her eyes against the blackness and it occurred to her that the lamp wasn't actually gone. It was still there, but there was something in front of it, a dark shape blocking out the light.

"Who's there?" she called out, panic rising in her voice. There was no reply. She could hear her heart beating loudly in her ears. What was that noise? Issie could hear something or someone moving towards her through the wet grass of the path above, coming closer and closer to the edge of the bank. She listened silently for a moment.

"Who's there?" she asked again. "Who is it?" Issie's heart was hammering in her ears, making it hard to think. There was the noise again! It wasn't footsteps at all! It was a horse, his hoofbeats making a soft thud on the grass above.

As the grey horse stepped forward to the edge of the path, a halo of light from the hurricane lamp surrounded him. Issie thought that he looked like an angel standing there above her. And he was an angel, her angel, come to save her when she needed him most. Issie felt her strength and determination returning. She wasn't alone any more. She had Mystic.

Still clinging on to the muddy bank with her left hand to stop herself from falling back down again, Issie reached out her other hand. She held her breath for a moment, almost afraid that if she actually tried to touch her pony, he would slip through her fingers like smoke.

But no. He was really there. Her aching fingers, covered in blood, blackberry prickles and mud, reached out and grasped on to the coarse strands of his shaggy mane.

The grey pony lowered his head so that Issie could reach out with her other hand. She knew what Mystic meant to do and she trusted him. She let go of the grass, but instead of falling backwards, she made a desperate grab with that hand too, hanging on to Mystic's neck. The pony took the strain of Issie's weight and backed up slowly on to the track, using the strength of his hindquarters to drag her with him, lifting Issie up, up, up until she was safely standing next to him on the track.

"Hey, Mystic," Issie murmured, throwing both arms around his neck, burying her face in his thick mane. "It's good to see you, boy."

Issie was so desperately pleased to see her horse, she wanted to just stay there like that, hugging him forever. But she had no time to waste. Hugs with her beloved pony would have to wait.

"We have to go now," she whispered. "Stardust needs us." Leading Mystic on to the track, she climbed up the other side, where the bank rose up a little. She was high up enough now to make a leap, throwing herself gracefully on to the pony's bare back. She felt the smoothness of Mystic's sleek dappled coat beneath her. She grabbed a hank of the gelding's thick mane. The bleeding from the blackberries had mostly stopped now and her hands didn't hurt so much any more. She grasped the mane tightly and tapped Mystic's sides with her heels.

"OK, Mystic, let's go!" she said, clucking him forward. Mystic gave a couple of trot strides and then began to canter down the track towards the film set. Issie felt the gentle rocking-horse motion of Mystic's canter and bent low over his neck as the pony picked his way along the darkened path through the inky blackness of the night.

On horseback at a canter it didn't take long to reach the bottom of the track. Straight ahead of her Issie could see the film crew crowded round. She felt sick. Was she too late? Her eyes searched frantically. Where were Angelique and Stardust?

Issie felt a surge of relief when she saw the vampire riders all gathered together on their black horses – and there was Stardust too! Eugene was still holding on to the palomino's bridle to stop her from bolting, which was just as well because Stardust looked completely spooked. So did Angelique. She was gripping the reins for dear life in two fists. She looked terrified. In front of her, Rupert was standing on a camera dolly and giving the riders their instructions.

"Right – we kick off here at the base of the mountain and we go all the way up the fortress to the castle in full gallop," Rupert said. "Angelique, let's give this scene lots of emotion. You are being chased by the vampires of Eleria. If they catch you, they're going to bite Seraphine and turn her against you. You are riding as if your life depends on it. OK?"

Angelique nodded, but Issie could see that she wasn't paying attention to anything Rupert was saying. She was too busy looking at the cobbled terrace steps that plateaued and then twisted and turned again, winding their way up the mountainside like a giant corkscrew towards the black castle. Even if Angelique had been a good rider, this was a dangerous stunt – the cobbles were slippery under the horses' hooves and the twisting track was bordered by a cold, hard stone wall on one side and a steep drop on the other. One step out of place and it would be all too easy to plummet in the darkness and fall to the rocks below.

"Rupert…" Angelique said with a shaky voice. "I have something I need to tell you…"

"What is it?" Rupert looked at the starlet. Angelique was about to speak when Eugene cut her off.

"Tell him later, Angel sweetheart! Rupert doesn't have time for this now, baby! Let's go!" And with that, Eugene gave Bob a quick nod and raised his camera into position on his shoulder. Issie saw Angelique's face turn deathly pale.

"No, wait! Stop! I don't want to—" She didn't get the chance to finish her sentence because, at that moment, Eugene pulled a sword out of the props chest next to him and lashed out, bringing the flat side of the blade down hard on Stardust's rump, letting go of the palomino's bridle at the same time.

Stardust, who was already wild-eyed with fear, felt the blow on her rump and immediately leapt forward as Angelique let out a terrified scream.

"Action!" Eugene shouted with a grin as Stardust bolted towards the first terrace. "Action!!"

Chapter 14

As Stardust galloped off with the screaming Angelique hanging on for dear life, Rupert rounded on Eugene. "You idiot! What do you think you're doing? We weren't ready! My cameras aren't even set up! It's not your job to shout action!"

Eugene ignored him and kept his own camera focused on the runaway palomino. "I'm getting great footage here, Rupert. Can we talk about this later?"

"Footage?!" Rupert fumed. "That horse is out of control! Angelique could be killed. That's it, Eugene! You will never work in Hollywood again. As of this moment you are banned from my set! Do you hear me? Banned!"

The men were so busy arguing that at first they didn't notice the second rider who had followed the runaway palomino up the citadel terraces at full gallop. Issie hadn't even stopped to think when she saw Stardust bolt. She had instantly kicked Mystic on, and the grey pony was already gaining on Angelique. They would reach the palomino before the first terrace, but would that be soon enough? How long could Angelique manage to stay on?

"Angelique! We're coming!" Issie shouted. A sudden gust of wind nearly drowned out her words, and then, as if from nowhere, the rain began to fall heavily.

What's going on? Issie wondered. The night sky above her was clear and starry. There hadn't even been so much as a breeze a few moments ago. *Where did this storm suddenly come from?*

The wind was howling around them now and the rain was so dense that Issie was already soaked to the skin. It all seemed so weird. *How come it isn't raining anywhere else?* Issie thought to herself. *It's only raining on us.*

She looked up. Above her, attached to the black stone walls of the mountain, out of view of the cameras, was the scaffolding that held the lights. Issie could see now that the scaffolding also held vast wind machines and sprinkler systems attached to enormous water pumps. This wasn't an ordinary storm – this was a movie storm! The film crew, who had been waiting in standby position, had seen the palomino coming up the mountain and must have thought they had missed their cue! They had leapt into action and cranked up the storm machines!

Not that it made any difference what was causing the storm. Issie was still soaked to the skin, and the cobblestones were slick with water and slippery beneath the horses' feet. Issie looked ahead and saw Stardust stumble. Angelique screamed again as she grabbed the mare's silver mane and hung on as the palomino miraculously regained her footing.

"Come on, Mystic," Issie clucked the grey pony on. "Now!" She had no time to lose. Angelique couldn't possibly hang on for much longer.

As they reached the cobblestoned plateau of the first terrace Mystic put on a burst of even greater speed. The little grey gelding came up alongside Stardust. Issie, crouched low like a jockey, kept one hand on Mystic's mane and reached over with the other to make a grab at Stardust's reins.

"What are you doing?" shrieked Angelique.

"Saving your life!" Issie snapped back. She grabbed at the reins again and this time she felt the leather in her hand. She closed her fingers and held on tight, making sure her other hand had a firm grip on Mystic's mane. This was a risky stunt. If Issie didn't get her timing right and Stardust pulled too hard, the mare could yank her right off Mystic's back and down on to the cobblestones below.

"Steady boy, whoa now," she called to the grey pony.

Mystic began to slow down, and as he did so Issie gave a hard tug on the reins to get Stardust's attention. The palomino seemed to understand immediately that Issie was in control, and didn't try to fight her. Issie had to be careful to slow Stardust down gently so that Angelique didn't get jolted out of the saddle. She spoke softly to the mare, making sure they stayed close to the safety of the high stone wall, away from the dangerous drop on the other side, as Stardust slowed down to a canter and then a trot. Finally, by the time they reached the second terrace, Issie had managed to steadily pull the palomino up to a total stop.

Issie leapt down from Mystic's back and held Stardust steady. The poor horse was shaking with fright. She had run purely out of fear when Eugene had hit her with the sword. Stardust had been just as terrified as Angelique.

"Easy, girl…" Issie cooed. Still clutching the saddle as if her life depended on it, Angelique looked pale and sick. Her knuckles were white from hanging on so tightly.

"Are you OK?" Issie asked.

Angelique nodded. She was trying not to cry.

"Do you want me to help you down?" Issie held out her hand to help and the starlet clambered down out of the saddle and fell to the ground, shaking and exhausted.

"Ohmygod, y'all!" she said as Issie helped her back up to her feet again. "That was the worst thing ever! I thought I was going to die!"

Tears were streaming down Angelique's cheeks and Issie could see that this time they were totally real. "Thank you," Angelique said, her voice still trembling. "That was amazing riding. I don't know what I'd have done if you hadn't—"

"Hey, hey, what's happening here?" Eugene suddenly emerged beside them out of the darkness. Bob, who was driving the motorcycle for him, was desperately trying to hang on to his sound boom and hold the handlebars at the same time. "Angelique! Baby, why did you stop?"

"Why did you hit Stardust?" Issie turned on Eugene, her face red with anger. "You spooked her! This is all your fault!"

"Hey, kid!" Eugene snapped back. "You stay out of this. That horse just needed a good whack to get her started, so I gave her one. I was helping!"

Suddenly the spotlights attached to the scaffolding above switched on, and Issie was blinded as the whole mountainside was bathed in a white glow. There was a dull whine like a plane engine dying as the motors that drove the wind machines began to slow down to a stop, and then she heard the sound of voices and footsteps coming up the hill towards them. Issie saw Rupert out in front of the others, running towards her and Angelique.

"Angelique! Are you OK?" he yelled out.

"I'm fine, Rupert!" Angelique called back, wiping her tears and pulling herself together. The director came running up the hill towards them.

"Are you sure you're OK?" he said, putting an arm around the shaking starlet.

"I'm OK," Angelique nodded.

Rupert looked around desperately. "Can I get a little help here? Now, please!"

Two of Angelique's assistants rushed forward with a blanket and some coffee and someone else brought out a chair which the starlet flopped down in.

"Angelique, you've been through quite enough for one night," Rupert said. "Why don't you go back to your trailer and get changed into some dry clothes?"

"Thanks, Rupert," Angelique said. She got unsteadily

to her feet as her assistants gathered around her and began to help her back down the mountainside.

Rupert turned to Eugene. "I thought I told you to get off my set!" he growled. Then he turned on Issie. "And what were you playing at?"

"Eugene hit Stardust so she bolted! I was trying to—" Issie began, but Rupert cut her off.

"Another night's filming ruined!" he fumed. "I don't really know what happened just now, but it seems pretty obvious. I've seen this before. You're a stunt double and you want attention. You want to be the star. Well, it's not going to happen, OK? So stop getting in the way."

"But… I was just…" Issie couldn't believe it! Why did Rupert always get the wrong end of the stick? It was like he deliberately wanted to blame Issie when all she was doing was helping. Rupert wasn't listening to Issie's explanation. He was looking around now with a puzzled expression on his face.

"Where is your horse?" he asked her.

"My horse?"

"The one you were riding when you stopped Angelique. The little grey. I didn't even know we had a grey on the set. The script doesn't call for one, does it?" Rupert began to leaf back through his director's notes, looking for the mention of a grey pony.

"Ummm…" Issie didn't know what to say. She had instinctively acted to save Angelique and Stardust. She hadn't even stopped to think about the fact that someone might see Mystic. In fact, she was kind of surprised that Rupert could see him.

Mystic was gone now of course. By the time Rupert and the crew had reached them, the little grey gelding was nowhere to be seen. He had disappeared up the mountain terrace as soon as Issie had dismounted to help Angelique.

"He's not actually in the script. The thing is I…" Issie began. But Rupert wasn't listening. He had lost interest in the whole Mystic matter. He was staring intently at the full moon above the castle. The clouds had cleared now and the night sky was sparkling with stars.

"Oh, brilliant!" Rupert shook his head. "A perfect full moon, everything is ready to go, the crew are all set, weather machines are working perfectly and now we don't have our star to ride the scene!" He looked at Issie, who was standing in front of him soaked to the skin and shivering in the chilly night air. "Will you do it?"

"Me?"

"Sure. You're Angelique's stunt double, aren't you? Well, this is her stunt. What do you say? Are you up for it?"

Issie looked at Stardust. The mare seemed to have calmed down now. Issie reached out her hand and stroked the palomino gently, running her hand down her velvety nose. "What do you say, girl? Want to go for a ride up to that castle?"

Stardust nickered back softly to her, and Issie knew then that the mare understood her. Stardust really trusted her.

"We're ready," Issie said to Rupert. "Let's do it."

The next thing Issie knew Rupert was barking orders and there was chaos on the set. Someone had thrust a script into Issie's hands. "You'll need to learn your lines," the assistant director told her. "But I'm not an actor!" Issie squeaked. "I'm just a stunt rider!"

"I know," the assistant director said. "You just need to speak the words to give us a marker. We'll redo the close-ups with Angelique in the studio against a blue screen later on." The assistant director grabbed the script back off Issie who was standing there staring blankly at it. "Here!" he said impatiently. "Page 126. This is your scene. Learn your lines. You've got five minutes!"

As Issie tried desperately to focus on the script, there was shouting and running as the props and lighting men got back into position and the weathermakers began to rev their engines. Then the costume and make-up department were swarming all over Issie, fitting a long blonde wig on her and pulling off her wet clothes to change her into a spare costume for Princess Galatea.

Meanwhile, at the base of the mountain terraces, the vampire riders were putting on their flowing robes and inserting their fake fangs once more in preparation for chasing her up the mountain.

"Isadora!" a voice called out to her. It was Aunt Hester running towards her with Stella and Kate close behind.

"Isadora! The girls told me what happened. Is Angelique all right?" Hester said.

"Uh-huh. I got to her in time and managed to stop Stardust. I think she's pretty shaken up," Issie said. "Aunty Hess, Angelique can't ride. That's what her big secret is. That's why she wouldn't get on Stardust the other day in the arena and that's why she pretended that Stardust stood on her foot. She's been doing anything she can to get off this movie because she's terrified of horses."

Hester looked shocked. "But she told Rupert that she was a great rider!"

"I know," Issie said, "but she's really not. Aunty Hess she doesn't know what she's doing. You mustn't let her ride Stardust again."

Suddenly a film crew runner appeared next to Issie. "Rupert is ready for you now, Miss Brown," the runner said. "Time to mount up."

"Wish me luck!" Issie smiled at her aunt as she swung herself up into Stardust's saddle.

"You're riding the castle chase?" Hester said. "Do you think Stardust is ready for this?"

Issie gave the palomino a firm pat on her glossy golden neck. "I know she is, Aunty Hess. Don't worry about us. Stardust is a star. Tonight we're going to prove it." And with that, Issie clucked the palomino into a canter and clattered off back down the cobblestoned path to the bottom of the hill where the rest of the riders were waiting to start the chase.

As the black hooded vampire riders gathered behind her ready to gallop up to the top of the citadel, Issie leant low and murmured to Stardust. "Hey, girl," she breathed softly. "Let's show them all what you can do."

"Take two… and… action!" Rupert shouted.

Issie and Stardust shot forward at a gallop, and as they did so the storm began to whirl around them. In the torrential rain, the vampire riders followed in their black, flowing robes. When they reached the third terrace, the black horses had surrounded the girl. The palomino tried to escape. She reared up, lashing out at the head vampire. The vampire drew back his hood to reveal his hideous white face. The palomino snorted in fear at the sight of him and the girl put her hand to the sword that lay on her hip, ready to unsheathe it.

"Leave her alone, Francis," Issie said. "You cannot possibly think you will win like this."

"Oh, but that is exactly what I think… Princess," Aidan replied with a lizard hiss in his voice. "Tonight we take Seraphine's life. She is the last of her kind. Your last hope. When she joins us and becomes one of the Horses of Darkness then you will have lost your kingdom forever."

Aidan jumped down from his black mount and stepped forward. He smiled, baring a set of long white fangs.

"Say goodnight, Seraphine," he said as he opened his mouth wide and lunged forward to plunge his fangs deep into the palomino's golden neck…

"And… cut!" Rupert shouted. The rain suddenly stopped and the studio lights flashed on, bathing everyone in a golden glow.

"Incredible! Nailed it in one take. That was terrific, everyone. It's a wrap!" There was a clapping and a whooping from the film crew at the news that the night's shooting was over. Issie jumped down off Stardust's back and gave her horse a huge hug. They had done it.

Later that night after they had put the horses away, the girls gathered together in Stella and Kate's room.

"I don't know why we're even having this meeting," Stella groaned. "I mean, it's all solved now, isn't it? So Angelique can't ride. Big deal. We know her big secret. She wanted to wriggle out of the movie so no one would know how useless she really is."

Issie shook her head. "I don't think it's that simple. I think someone has been trying to make a fool of Angelique all along." She paused. "I'm sure someone is deliberately causing trouble for Angelique. And that means Stardust is in danger – and so will I be if I have to ride Angelique's stunts from now on. I've thought of a way we can try and trap whoever is doing this, but we'll need help."

"Issie!" Stella said. "Of course we'll help."

"Thanks, Stella," Issie said, "but I didn't mean you. I mean we'll need help from someone else – and she's not going to like it…"

"I cannot believe you're asking me this!" Natasha glared at Issie. "After all this time, leaving me out of everything and being horrible to me, and now you want me to join your poxy little gang?"

Stella couldn't stand this. "Us being horrible? You're the one who's a complete—"

"Shhh, Stella! Let's not get into a fight about who did what." Issie tried to calm her down. Then she turned her attention to Natasha who was standing in front of the three girls with her arms crossed defiantly.

"Natasha," Issie said carefully, "I know that things haven't been great between us since we got here. But this isn't just about us. I think Stardust and Angelique are in danger. We need your help. I've told you my plan. Now what do you say?"

Natasha looked at Stella, Kate and Issie. She didn't say anything for a moment and then when she did finally speak her voice sounded high and nervous.

"If I do this, Stella is not allowed to make fun of me any more – ever. OK?" Stella bristled at this. She was about to say something, but Issie shot her a look.

"Yes, Natasha. Stella is OK with that. She promises."

"You know, it's not like I'm trying to be one of your dumb gang or anything…"

"Oh, what-ever!" Stella rolled her eyes. "Are you going to do it or not?"

"There!" Natasha pointed at Stella. "That's just what I mean! She is always being mean to me! Well, that's it! Forget it!" She stormed off towards her bedroom.

"What? I didn't do anything!" Stella protested.

"Stella!" Issie said. "Why do you always have to wind her up?"

"I don't!" Stella protested. "Anyway, do we really need Stuck-up Tucker for this? Can't we do it with just the three of us?"

"You know we can't, Stella. We need Natasha to make it look convincing," Issie sighed. "I'd better go in there and talk to her."

Issie found Natasha lying face down on the bed with her head in the pillows. "Go away!" she said without looking up.

"Natasha. Look, I'm really sorry. Stella is just like that. She didn't mean to upset you." Natasha pulled her face out of the pillows and Issie could see that she had been crying.

"You didn't tell her, did you? About my mum and dad splitting up? She'd be just awful to me if she knew. It's horrible at home at the moment – Mummy couldn't wait to drop me off here again to get rid of me. And then I get here and Stella is so awful to me..."

"I haven't told anyone," Issie said. "You asked me not to tell anyone and I haven't. And I'm sure your mum wasn't trying to get rid of you. And Stella, well, actually maybe Stella *is* trying to get rid of you..." Natasha almost smiled at this. "...but she can't, because we need you," Issie smiled back. "Come on, Natasha. Will you help us with our plan? Stardust really needs your help."

"OK," Natasha sniffled. "I guess I might as well help since I'm stuck here. After all, I'm not doing anything else, am I?"

"Thanks!" Issie grinned. "Tomorrow night then!"

Natasha nodded. "Tomorrow night."

"I can't believe you convinced Natasha!" Stella was amazed when Issie returned with the news.

"I know!" Issie said. "Now there's just one more person we need to get onboard if this is going to work."

"Issie, do you think she'll do it?"

"She has to," Issie said gravely. "Our plan depends on it."

Chapter 15

After a late night spent filming at the castle, Hester was surprised to find all her riders in the arena bright and early the next morning. Issie, Kate, Stella and Natasha were mounted up and kitted out in their back protectors and helmets, ready to start training.

"I didn't schedule a session for this morning, did I?" Hester was confused. "I thought I told you girls you could sleep in."

"You did," Kate said, "but we woke up early and thought we might as well get some extra practice."

"We want to try the obstacle course one more time," Stella said. "If that's OK?"

"Of course it is," Hester smiled. "Anything in particular that you want to practise?"

"Yes, actually," Natasha said. "We'd like to practise our swordfighting – you know, with the straw dummies?"

Hester nodded. "Good idea. We still have the big battle scene coming up. An extra rehearsal to practise your swordplay wouldn't hurt. You girls saddle up your palominos and I'll go and get the swords."

By the time the girls had tacked up and led their horses back into the arena, Hester had been to the props chest in the tack room and grabbed them each a broadsword. "Remember, just because these are only made of hardwood doesn't mean they aren't dangerous," Hester said as she handed out the swords. "They're not the real thing, obviously, but you could still do some damage with them."

"That's what we were thinking," Stella said.

"I beg your pardon, dear?" Hester said. "What did you say?"

"Ummm, she meant that they're dangerous and that's why we have to be careful," Issie said, giving Stella a look.

Stella shrugged and took her sword. "Well, come on then. Are we going to start fighting or are we just going to stand here all day?"

The girls rode over to the far side of the arena where Aunt Hester's obstacle course finished with the row of straw men tied to posts. The straw men all had red bullseyes on their chests.

"You girls have practised this at a trot and a canter already," Hester said. "I think you're ready to run through it at a gallop."

Issie, Natasha, Stella and Kate lined up on their horses about twenty metres away from their row of straw opponents. "Now, you carry your swords like this, with the blades pointed upwards as you ride," Hester explained, swinging the sword in broad strokes over her head. "Then use the flat of your blade like this to whack against the opponent, or if you want to go in for the kill, drive the point home like this!" She demonstrated by piercing the bullseye on the straw dummy with her own blade.

"Are you ready?" Hester asked. "Get set... charge!"

The four palominos leapt forward in full gallop, the girls waving their broadswords high above their heads. As they bore down on the straw men, each of them lowered their sword and struck a blow.

"I got him!" Stella squealed. "I totally got him."

"Me too!" Natasha said as she pulled Rosie up to a halt.

"I think I missed," Issie sighed as she turned Stardust around and trotted back towards the others.

"Well, we'd better try again then," Stella said.

"You can't afford to miss, Issie, not tonight."

"Tonight?" Hester looked confused. "What do you mean? We're not shooting tonight. The battle scene is being shot in the daylight, Stella – Rupert has scheduled it for tomorrow."

"Ummm," Stella said, "I guess I got mixed up." She smiled at the others. "Shall we go again? I want to get another bullseye!"

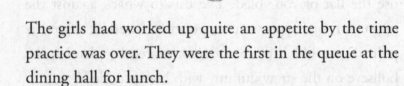

The girls had worked up quite an appetite by the time practice was over. They were the first in the queue at the dining hall for lunch.

"Look," Stella said as they were sitting down at their table. "There's Angelique." The starlet was over at the buffet, complaining loudly to her assistants. "I can't eat any of this! You know I'm only allowed a wheatgrass shot and mung beans! Get the chef to sort it out now!"

Issie stood up. "OK, wish me luck. I'm going to go talk to her."

"Wait!" Natasha said. "Maybe I should do it. Angelique is my friend. She'll listen to me."

Issie nodded. "OK. Let's both talk to her together."

"Good luck!" Stella and Kate said. They sat and watched as Issie and Natasha walked over to the blonde starlet.

"Can you hear what they're saying?" Stella asked.

"Uh-uh." Kate shook her head. "But they're talking to her. I can see Angelique nodding."

By the time Issie and Natasha returned to the table the girls were desperate. "What did she say? What did she say?" Stella was about to burst.

"It's done. She's in." Issie said.

The girls finished their meals, but they didn't leave the dining room. They continued to sit there in silence, their eyes glued on Angelique.

"Can I sit with you guys?" It was Aidan.

Stella gave him an anxious glance. "Yeah, yeah. Whatever. Hurry up and sit then! And don't say anything."

"What?" Aidan was confused. "Hey, what's going on here? Why aren't you guys talking to each other?"

"Shhhh, Aidan! Be quiet!" Issie hissed. "We're trying to listen to Angelique."

Over at the blonde starlet's table Angelique was holding court. Her entourage were all gathered around, attending to her needs and hanging off her every word. Suddenly the whole table fell silent as Rupert arrived in the dining hall.

"Rupert! Hi, y'all!" Angelique called out, waving frantically to the director. "Come over here and sit down and have some lunch with me!"

Rupert looked a little uncomfortable with this idea, but he nodded and sent his assistant over to the buffet to get him some food while he sat down at the table with Angelique. Angelique's entourage leapt up and moved out of the way to make a space for the director.

"Rupert." Angelique smiled her brightest, whitest smile at the director. "I was just telling everyone here that I feel simply dreadful about last night. You know, it gave me such a shock when that horse bolted. That's why my performance was so bad." Angelique batted her eyelashes at Rupert and smiled again. "I know I can make it up to you. I'm going to be, like, totally ready to ride my own stunts in the battle scene tomorrow. And to make sure I'm ready, I'm going to practise tonight."

"You are?" Rupert raised an eyebrow.

"Uh-huh," Angelique said. "No cameras or anything though, OK, Rupert? I just want to ride up to the castle by myself and practise. I need to get psyched. I think a little bit of time by myself with my horse will do the trick. I'm going to go up there alone when it gets dark."

Rupert nodded at this. "I think that's a really good

idea, Angelique. I'll tell the stables to get a horse ready for you this evening – and we can get the crew to leave the lighting rig switched on up at the castle. You go rehearse as much as you like—"

Rupert stopped in mid-sentence and turned around. There, behind him, was Eugene with his camera whirring and Bob holding the sound boom.

"What the... what are you two idiots still doing here?" Rupert's face was like thunder. "I thought I kicked you off my film set?"

"Rupert, baby, don't be like that—" Eugene began, but Rupert cut him down with an icy glare.

"I said leave my film set NOW!"

"Angelique?" Eugene pleaded. "Can you put in a good word for us? You want us to stay, don't you?"

"Sorry, y'all," Angelique said. "It's Rupert's decision." She made a telephone shape with her fingers. "I'll call you, OK? Bye bye now! Love your work!"

"All right, all right. We were just leaving," Eugene said flatly. "Come on, Bob. We're out of here."

Rupert turned to his assistant. "Tell security I want those two banned from the set. I don't want them bothering Angelique any more."

Angelique stood up. "Well, I'd better get going too! I

have a Pilates lesson with my trainer in my trailer," she said. There was a sudden shuffling of chairs as her entourage all stood up to follow her. Angelique flicked her hair back and blew Rupert a kiss over her shoulder as she left. "See y'all later!"

The girls all watched Angelique leave. And then, finally, Aidan spoke. "What's going on here, girls?"

Stella, Kate and Natasha all looked at Issie. "Should we tell him?" Stella asked her. Issie nodded.

"Tell me what?" Aidan was confused. "Issie, what is going on?"

"I can't talk about it here!" Issie hissed to him. "Meet us at the stables. Tonight."

That night, the moon was full once more. At the top of the black mountain, the castle made a grim silhouette against the night sky. As promised, Rupert had asked the crew to leave the lights on. The bulbs flickered like a thousand candles shining out of the tiny windows in the turrets and cast an eerie glow in the castle courtyard. While the courtyard and towers of the castle glowed, the cobbled path that circled up the mountainside was much more dimly lit. It was so dark on the mountain terraces that it took a moment to see the rider coming up the path in the moonlight.

Angelique Adams rode slowly up the cobbled tracks on her palomino. She was dressed in her Princess Galatea costume, a white gossamer shirt and sky-blue jodhpurs. Her long blonde hair tumbled loose over her shoulders and shone in the moonlight. Her sword hung at her hip.

When Angelique reached the first terrace she halted the horse and looked around, then set off again along the dark path that wound up and around to the peak of the mountain fortress to the castle gates. When she reached the gates, she hesitated once more, as if uncertain whether to enter. She stood at the drawbridge, holding her horse steady for what seemed like ages.

What was she waiting for?

Then, from the terraces below, came the clean chime of horseshoes on cobblestones as another rider approached the castle. Angelique was not alone. Someone had followed her.

Galloping up the terraced steps came a black horse. His rider, who was crouched low over the horse's neck, was hidden beneath the black hooded cloak of a vampire rider. The black rider rounded the third terrace and urged his horse to gallop faster as they closed in on their quarry, the horse's hoofbeats pounding their rhythm on the cobblestones. The palomino and her rider remained frozen, watching as the black horseman got closer and closer, waiting to see what would happen next.

When the hooded rider was just a few metres away from the girl and the palomino, he pulled the black horse to a sudden halt. He reached into the folds of his black cloak and grasped the broadsword that was hidden beneath his robes. In one swift movement he unsheathed the sword and held it high above his head so that it glinted in the moonlight.

The girl's face grew pale with horror as she realised what the hooded rider meant to do. He was going to attack her! In a sudden rush, the black rider charged down on Angelique with his sword aimed straight at her. As he did so, the girl wheeled the palomino swiftly around and urged her on at a gallop over the drawbridge and through the castle gate into the stone courtyard, with the black rider following hard on her heels.

The castle courtyard was vast and every corner was shrouded in shadows. The girl on the palomino had disappeared into the gloom and the black rider began to ride the perimeter of the courtyard, searching out the shadowy nooks, looking for his prey. Suddenly, from the opposite side of the courtyard, a girl on a palomino rode forward. Her blonde hair shone in the glow of the courtyard lights. She looked at the black rider and smiled as she put her hand to her hip and pulled out her own broadsword.

"Looking for me, y'all?" she asked.

"No!" came another voice from behind the black rider. "He's looking for me."

The rider in the black hood wheeled his horse around. Right behind him was another girl. She looked exactly the same – with long blonde hair and the clothes of Princess Galatea. This girl also rode a palomino and held a broadsword in her hand.

"Actually," a third voice came from the shadows at the other side of the courtyard, "I think you'll find that he's looking for me." Another rider, once again blonde and brandishing a broadsword, rode forward on her palomino.

The hooded rider began to yank his horse about viciously by the reins, circling this way and that, unsure of which way to turn as the three palominos closed in on him. Then, from behind him, he heard yet another voice.

"No. You're all wrong. It's me he's after." A fourth identical rider came forward, holding her sword high over her head so that its blade pointed straight up to the sky.

"I suppose you're wondering which one of us is Angelique?" the fourth rider said. Then she reached up and pulled off her blonde wig, exposing the long dark hair underneath. At the same time two of the other riders pulled off their own wigs and now it was plain to see that the riders were none other than Issie, Stella and Kate. The only blonde left was the girl the hooded rider had chased up the terraces to the castle gates, and he spun his horse around to face her.

"Sorry to disappoint you," Natasha shrugged. "My blonde hair might be real, but I'm not Angelique either." She drew out her broadsword.

"OK," Issie said, "that's enough. It's all over. You can't escape now, so you may as well give up."

The black rider sat perfectly still on his horse, neither speaking nor moving a muscle. Then, without any warning, he rode towards Issie, trying to get past her to escape through the castle gates.

Issie was ready for him. She kicked Stardust on and came back at the black rider, her sword propped at her hip like a jousting lance as she rode. As the horses met, the hooded rider swung his sword, but Issie pulled Stardust to one side, avoiding his blow, and the hooded rider's sword cut through thin air.

"Hey, leave her alone!" Stella called. She rode forward, swinging the blade at her side as if it were a cowgirl's lasso.

Before the hooded rider even had a chance to turn around she had struck him a glancing blow across his right arm. The black horseman cried out in pain. It was the first time the man had uttered a sound. Now he was silent once more as he turned his horse around and rode back into the middle of the courtyard, surveying his four foes.

"Look out, Natasha!" Stella shouted as the black rider rode desperately at her, barging past her and riding hard towards the castle gates.

"Aidan! Now!" Issie called out. There was the grinding and clanking of heavy metal chains as Aidan, who had been hiding behind the castle gates the whole time, turned the winch and released the huge iron portcullis. The vast rusty metal grille that hung suspended over the castle gates suddenly creaked into life and began to lower shut, blocking the castle entrance.

"He's going to make it in time!" Stella yelled.

"No, he's not!" Issie said.

She was right. The portcullis rattled down in front of the black rider, forcing his horse to stop. He turned to face the girls once more, raising his sword. Then he seemed to think better of it, dropped the sword instead and pulled back his hood. Sitting on the horse in front of them, looking rather embarrassed in his black robes, was Bob the sound man.

"Aw, for krissakes, Bob! What did you have to go and do that for? I was getting amazing footage and you ruined everything!" Eugene Sneadly ran forward out of the darkness with his video camera and glared up at Bob. Eugene still had his camera rolling as Bob dismounted from the horse.

"No, Eugene," he said. "You're the one who has ruined everything. You've always ruined it. You told me to get on the horse and ride after Angelique to give her a fright. Well, it's all backfired. Just like everything you do. Don't you get it? I quit. It's over."

Bob reached out and took the camera from Eugene's hands. In the dark outside the castle gates, footsteps could be heard approaching the huge gates of the castle's portcullis. He was right. It was over.

Chapter 16

At first when the others arrived Eugene had refused to admit to anything. "It didn't matter, though," Issie told Hester afterwards, "because Bob blabbed the whole story – he told them everything."

"You'd better explain this all to me again. I still don't understand," Aunt Hester said. The night's adventures were over now and they were all gathered together back at the barracks, the girls snuggled together under rugs on the sofa with mugs of hot chocolate.

"Eugene was deliberately causing trouble the whole time. He did it all for the sake of his stupid documentary," Issie said. "Angelique's supposed to be this big drama queen, but it turns out her real life just wasn't dramatic enough for Eugene. So he decided to make it a bit more exciting."

"That was why he wanted her to ride so desperately that day at the ridge," Stella added. "But then Angelique made all that fuss about Stardust standing on her foot…"

"So Eugene didn't know that she couldn't ride?" Hester asked.

"Uh-uh," Issie shook her head. "He couldn't figure out why his star kept disappearing and refusing to get on a horse. He wasn't trying to hurt Angelique. He just wanted a bit more action for his documentary. When Angelique kept coming up with excuses and refusing to do the stunts, Eugene got more and more desperate to create some drama. His last two films have been flops. This documentary was his last chance."

"How did you manage to set him up?" Hester asked Issie.

"Angelique helped us. She told everyone in the canteen that she'd be riding by herself tonight up at the castle. It worked – Eugene totally believed her. I guess after Rupert threw them off the set this was his last chance. So he made Bob pretend to be a vampire rider. He was never going to hurt Angelique or anything. He was only trying to spook her to get some controversial footage for his documentary."

"Bob thought he was following Angelique up to the

castle. Only it wasn't really her – it was me!" Natasha grinned. "It was Issie's idea. I look the most like Angelique. It wasn't until Bob got close and saw all four of us that he realised he'd made a mistake, and by then it was too late!"

"That was so cool when he chased you into the courtyard," Stella grinned. "He must have been so confused when he saw the rest of us in our wigs. Four Angeliques!"

"How about when you totally got him with your broadsword, Stella?" Kate giggled.

Hester raised an eyebrow. "So that's why you all wanted to practise your swordfighting! Riding about with swords in the middle of the night! What were you thinking? I wish you had let me in on this ridiculous plan," she said sternly.

"Would you have let us go through with it if we'd told you, Aunty Hess?" Issie said.

"Of course not!" Hester harrumphed.

"That's why we didn't tell you!" Issie grinned. The others all laughed.

"As for you!" Hester glared at Aidan. "I can't imagine what possessed you to go along with them."

"It's not his fault, Aunty Hess," Issie pleaded. "We

only told him at the last minute and he had to help us."

All this time, Strudel, Nanook and Taxi had been lying peacefully at Hester's feet. Suddenly they leapt up and began to head for the front door.

"Down! Stay!" Hester instructed the dogs.

"Is it OK to come in?" the voice outside the door asked nervously. Issie looked up and saw the last person she expected to lay eyes on.

Angelique Adams didn't have her usual entourage following her around. She was all alone. "Umm, are those dogs really safe?" she asked.

"They're perfectly safe. Come in, Angelique!" Hester smiled. Angelique smiled back and edged past the dogs over to the sofa where the girls were sitting.

"So," Stella said, "you're scared of dogs… and horses?"

Angelique nodded. She stood next to the sofa looking rather uncomfortable. "Hey, what's that y'all are drinking?" She peered into Stella's mug.

"Umm, hot chocolate?" Stella said.

Angelique eyed up the mug hungrily and sighed. "My nutritionist will only let me drink wheatgrass shots."

Hester smiled. "Well, your nutritionist isn't here now, dear. Would you like a nice cup of hot chocolate?"

"Yeah. Get me some," Angelique said. Then she

looked embarrassed as she realised she was being rude. "I mean, yes, *thanks*, Hester. That would be great."

"Sit down and make yourself comfy on the sofa next to the girls," Hester said. "I'll put the milk on."

Angelique smiled at Issie and Stella who both moved over to make room for her on the sofa. She sat quietly between them while Hester made her hot chocolate. Then, when she had the hot mug in her hands, she finally spoke.

"I never meant to lie, you know, about being able to ride. I never even wanted to do this stupid movie. I am, like, sooo scared of horses! But Rupert is the hottest director in Hollywood and Malcolm, my agent, said this film would be the big one. It might even win me an Oscar. He told me riding would be really easy. And then once I got here and I realised how scary it was, well, I tried to get out of doing the movie but by then it was too late. And Eugene kept harassing me. He said he wanted me to ride so that he'd have all this 'amazing footage' for his documentary."

Angelique stared at her mug. "I feel so stupid. I can't believe I trusted him. He didn't care if I got hurt or looked stupid, as long as I was a drama queen for his dumb ol' film..." she said miserably.

"It's so hard when you live like I do. I know it looks

like I have lots of friends because I'm, like, famous. But they're not my friends at all really – they're just people who work for me. I thought Eugene was my friend, and now I find out he was just using me."

Angelique paused as she looked around at the four girls sitting next to her. She smiled at them. "Y'all don't know how lucky you are. I wish I had friends like you, real friends that I could really depend on."

The girls were all silent for a moment. It was Natasha who finally spoke. "You do," she said, smiling back. "You've got us."

The news of what happened that night at the black castle spread fast. By the morning, when the girls turned up on set, the whole crew gave them a standing ovation. Leading the cheering was Rupert, who came straight up to Issie and shook her vigorously by the hand.

"Isadora, I'm afraid I've had the wrong end of the stick all along," he said. "I was a bit of an idiot really. I didn't know Angelique couldn't ride. And when Stardust stood on her foot, I had no reason not to believe her." Rupert sighed. "Angelique has explained everything to me and now it all makes sense. I can see that you were only trying to help…" He looked Issie in the eyes. "I misjudged you, Isadora, and I'm sorry. It won't happen again."

Issie smiled. "That's OK," she said.

"Well, it's over now!" Rupert said, resuming his normal brisk demeanour. He let go of Issie's hand and gave Stardust a firm pat on the neck. "Right! Shall we get started then?" He turned around to address the rest of his crew.

"All right, everyone!" he called out. "I think that's enough fuss. We've got a film to finish. Can I have everyone in their places, please?"

"Princess Galatea!" a deep voice growled. Issie turned around and saw a hooded rider coming up towards her on a black horse. "Are you ready to do battle?" The rider pulled back his black hood and revealed a bald head covered with purple veins.

"Ohmygod! Aidan!" Issie giggled.

"If you can do battle in the castle fortress in the middle of the night then this should be a piece of cake for you," Aidan grinned. "A battle scene at the castle in broad daylight."

Issie raised her sword in front of her and looked Aidan in the eye. "Bring it on!" she laughed.

"Everybody mount up!" Rupert called from his

director's chair on top of the camera crane. "I want the palomino riders with Galatea on standby outside the castle gates please!"

"I'll see you in battle!" Aidan smiled at her. "Try not to hit me too hard with your sword when we're fighting, OK?" He slipped his fake fangs into his mouth and gave her an evil grin. "Or I might be forced to bite you!"

Issie smiled back, then she wheeled her palomino mare around and cantered over to Stella, Kate and Natasha, who were already in position waiting at the castle gate.

"Vampire riders should all be in the courtyard now please! Final positions, everyone!" Rupert shouted through his loudhailer. The crew on the set went dead quiet as Rupert raised his hand and then pointed straight at Issie. "And... action!"

That was Issie's cue. She raised her sword to the sky and cantered Stardust forward to the middle of the drawbridge. Stardust, who had been waiting for Issie's signal, responded immediately when Issie tightened the reins, rearing straight up on her hind legs and letting out a loud whinny as she thrashed her hooves in the air. As Stardust came back down to the ground, Issie held the mare steady.

"You're through, Francis! I'm taking back my kingdom!" she said. Then she pointed her sword straight at the head vampire. "And I'm taking my horses back too!" And with those words, the golden palomino charged.

In the end, the battle would be swift and violent. Well, at least the final filmed version would be. But the truth of making movies is that nothing happens quickly. In fact, the battle scene took all day to film and by the time the girls arrived at the dining hall that evening they were all exhausted.

"My arm hurts from waving my sword over my head!" Kate groaned.

"I can't believe we had to shoot that same bit where I hit that vampire with my sword, like, ten times!" Stella grumbled.

"Sounds like my Daredevil riders need to toughen up!" Hester said, looking around the table at them.

"Not me!" Natasha said indignantly. "I wasn't even complaining."

"Well, dear," said Hester, grinning at her, "that just proves there's a first time for everything!"

As the girls went back to the buffet for second helpings of chocolate cake and whipped cream, Aidan came running into the dining hall.

"Issie!" He was trying to catch his breath to get the words out. "You've got to come… with me… we've got to go! Now!"

"But I was just going to have some more dessert!" Issie objected.

"No time!" Aidan wheezed. "I've got the truck outside. We need to leave straightaway!" Issie looked confused.

"Aidan? What's wrong?"

Aidan bent down with his hands on his knees, trying once and for all to get his breath back. Then he took a deep gulp of air and looked at Issie. "It's Blaze," he said. "She's having her foal."

Chapter 17

Issie's heart was pounding as she leapt out of the horse truck and ran across the gravel driveway to the front door of Avery's cottage.

"Tom?" she called out as she ran through the house. "Tom! Where are you?"

Issie tore through the kitchen and was heading for the back door when she ran straight into Avery who was bent over taking off his gumboots.

"Issie! You nearly ran me over," Tom grinned. "I wasn't expecting you to get here so quickly."

"Tom!" Issie's voice was strained with panic. "Where is she? Is she OK? I knew I shouldn't have left her. It's all my fault and now I've missed everything…"

"Hey, hey, calm down," Avery smiled. "It's OK. She hasn't had the foal yet, Issie."

Issie felt a wave of relief at this news. "Ohmygod, I was so worried! Aidan told me that you said to come straightaway and I thought…"

Avery shook his head. "I should have told Aidan not to worry you. I wanted you to come back because she's showing signs of foaling, but she's not in labour yet," Avery continued. "I've just checked her again now and I think it's probably going to be another forty-eight hours at least before anything happens."

He smiled at Issie. "Do you want to see her? She's in the paddock next to the house. I haven't moved her into the stable – the weather's been so lovely she's better off grazing outside."

Issie followed Avery out of the house. The paddocks behind his farm cottage were neatly fenced with dark-stained wooden rails. In the paddock closest to the house, standing under the shade of a magnolia tree, a chestnut mare with a flaxen mane and tail and a white blaze was grazing peacefully.

Issie gave a whistle and Blaze raised her head. Her ears pricked forward as Issie whistled again. Blaze nickered a greeting in return as she began to walk towards her owner. Issie watched her wobble along, her enormous belly swinging from side to side. The mare had grown so much in the past week. There was no doubt about it – she was ready to foal.

"She's been restless. She keeps lying down and then standing up again, but nothing is under way yet," Avery said.

"Hey, girl," Issie cooed softly to the mare. She gave Blaze a pat on her glossy neck and examined her. Issie peered at the little black box that was strapped on to the halter underneath Blaze's jaw.

"The foaling monitor's rigged to this pager," Avery said, gesturing to a second, smaller black box that was attached to his jacket pocket. "It will let us know the minute she goes into labour." He handed Issie the pager. "Now that you're back, why don't you hang on to it?"

Issie took the pager from Avery and held it in her hands as if it were a precious jewel. She looked up at her riding instructor. "Tom, I... I don't want to leave her again. I mean, I don't want to go home. I know my house isn't far from here, but what if she has the foal and I don't make it back here in time? What if I miss it?"

Avery nodded. "I'll call your mum and organise for

her to bring over a change of clothes. You'll stay here tonight in the spare room."

"Thanks, Tom," Issie said with relief.

"We'll phone her right now," Avery said, "and then I want to hear all about how things went with Stardust once you were back on the set. No more dramas, I hope?"

Issie laughed. "I wouldn't say that exactly. Actually, there was a lot of drama. It's a long story…" Issie told her instructor everything.

"Stardust was great, though, Tom. She wasn't scared of swords or anything and she acted like a real star."

"So filming has finished?" Avery asked.

"They've still got to film all the close-ups with the real actors. Hester has been coaching Angelique, giving her private lessons," Issie said. "Angelique won't be riding any stunts obviously, but at least she'll be brave enough to sit on Stardust while they film her close-ups and finish the movie."

At this point, Aidan, who had parked the horse truck and joined them, couldn't wait any longer. "Come on, Issie! Hurry up! You haven't told Avery the best bit yet. Tell him about Stardust."

"Oh yes!" Issie grinned. "I was really worried that Stardust would end up with some horrible trainers again on her next job, but Hester says she's spoken to Stardust's owners and they've agreed to sell her! Hester has bought her off them. Aidan will take Stardust back to Blackthorn Farm as soon as the film wraps. So now Blackthorn Farm has three palominos!"

The doorbell rang at that moment and Mrs Brown came in. "Ohhh, it's good to have you home in one piece!" she said, racing over and snuggling Issie up in a big bear hug.

"Muuum! Get off!" Issie said, shrugging off her mum, embarrassed to be getting made a fuss of in front of Avery and Aidan.

"Right then," said Mrs Brown as Avery brought out the scones and jam to go with the tea, and Aidan and Issie began to wolf them down. "I want to hear all the gossip! Did you get to meet any celebrities? What is Angelique Adams really like?"

"At first I thought she was a spoilt Hollywood brat," Issie said, "but once you get to know her she's OK..." She reached for another scone.

"I hear she's a very good rider!" Mrs Brown said.

Issie laughed. "Actually, Mum, I had to help her out with that bit."

"Well, at least you're back home without any slings or

bandages this time. You obviously managed to keep out of trouble for once," Mrs Brown said.

"Really?" Avery said as he plonked the teapot down on the table. "It sounds like there was quite a bit of trouble – especially that swordfight with Eugene."

Issie shot Avery a look as if to say, "Be quiet!" but it was too late. Mrs Brown raised an eyebrow.

"Swordfight? What swordfight? Isadora, what is he talking about?!"

Issie spent the next hour trying to explain herself to her mum, a task which left her totally exhausted. At least it seemed to go OK and Mrs Brown calmed down in the end. Issie thought it was a good sign when her mother offered to stay and help Avery make dinner for them all. She even made Issie's favourite meal – cottage pie.

"Does this mean you're not angry with me?" Issie beamed between mouthfuls.

"It means you looked like you needed a good square meal," Mrs Brown said, frowning at her. "As for being angry with you, I haven't decided yet. The whole thing sounds so outrageous, I don't know what to think. I do know that your aunt will be getting an earful from me – but then what else is new?" she sighed, her frown thawing out into a smile.

After her mum had left, Issie went to bed early with grand plans to read the last chapter of the book Avery had bought for her, *The Care of the Mare and Foal*. But after just a couple of pages she found she couldn't keep her eyes open. As she drifted off to sleep she checked the pager which sat on the table beside her bed. The red light indicated that it was switched on, but nothing was happening, so Issie snuggled under the duvet and instantly fell into a deep sleep.

The night had been calm when Issie went to bed, but now a storm was coming. The wind had picked up and the rain was falling heavily. Issie felt herself getting soaked to the skin, goosebumps prickling all over as the drops of rain fell. What was she doing outside in the rain? What was going on? She was so wet and cold, she was shaking. Her body was chilled to the bone and the rain kept running into her eyes, blurring her vision and making it impossible to see. She tried to concentrate, to focus on the shapes in front of her – she could make out a black hooded figure in the rain, and a grey shadow moving about in Blaze's paddock.

"Who's there?" she shouted. "Mystic? Is that you? Where is Blaze? Is she in trouble, Mystic? Mystic!" she screamed out. "Where are you? What's happening?"

Mystic whinnied back to her. His cry was loud and shrill, so loud that it rose above the noise of the storm. So loud that it woke her up.

Issie sat bolt upright. She wasn't outside in the paddock at all! She was still in bed. She had been dreaming. But it didn't feel like a dream at all. It had been so real. She lay there shivering, her body cold and clammy with sweat, still half asleep, trying to figure out what her dream meant.

Her thoughts were shattered by the shrill whinny of a horse. It was the same chilling cry that had woken her from her sleep.

Mystic! She threw herself out of bed. If Mystic was here then there was no doubt that Blaze was in trouble. Issie looked at the bedside table where the pager was sitting. Nothing. The foaling alarm hadn't gone off. Never mind – she trusted Mystic more than some foaling alarm. Issie ran for the back door, pulling on her gumboots.

When she opened the door she could see that the storm had not been a dream after all. It was howling a gale and the rain was pelting down. She stepped back inside and grabbed Avery's huge black hooded jacket off the coat hook, pulling it on as she ran out into the darkness towards Blaze's paddock.

"Mystic!" Issie yelled out. Her voice was swept away by the storm. She was about to shout out again when Mystic suddenly appeared in the paddock right in front of her. The grey horse was dripping wet from the rain. Issie reached out over the rails and grabbed a handful of his coarse mane. It felt like damp rope in her fingers.

"Come on," she said, unbolting the gate to Blaze's paddock to join him. "We've got to get to Blaze."

Shutting the gate behind her, Issie climbed up the gate rungs and leapt on to Mystic's back. She hadn't counted on the rain making the grey horse so slippery. It was hard to stay on bareback and Issie found herself sliding as Mystic cantered across the paddock towards the magnolia tree at the far side. She knew that this was the fastest way to find Blaze, so she wrapped her hands in Mystic's mane, tightened her legs around the little grey and held on.

The rain was so heavy now and it was so dark that at first when they reached the tree, she couldn't see Blaze at all. Finally she could make out the shape of a pony sheltering up against the tree, her head hung low as she tried to avoid the worst of the weather.

As Issie slid down off Mystic's back and ran over to the mare she could see something was wrong. Blaze was turning her head back and forth as if she were sniffing at her flank with her nose.

She's in labour. The foal is coming, Issie thought. *Why hasn't the foaling alarm gone off?*

All she knew was that if Mystic hadn't woken Issie up, Blaze would have had her foal out here alone in the storm – and in this weather the foal could easily die. Issie shivered as she felt the rain soaking through her coat. The chill snapped her into action. Blaze was still in danger. She had to move quickly.

Issie looked back through the rain at the farmhouse. Should she run and get Avery and Aidan? There wasn't time. She would have to get the mare inside by herself.

"Come on, girl!" She grabbed Blaze's halter and pulled. But Blaze refused to move. The mare didn't want to leave the shelter of the magnolia tree and go out into the rain, and the pains in her belly were telling her to stay where she was.

"Blaze!" Issie cried, yanking on the halter. "Come on! We have to get you inside!" Issie could feel herself becoming more and more distressed as Blaze pulled back and refused to move. "Come on, girl!" she pleaded.

This wasn't going to work! Issie let go of the halter. She turned to the grey gelding standing next to her. "Mystic, I can't move her," she said. "You have to help me."

The grey pony seemed to understand. He walked behind Blaze and nudged at the mare with his nose. Blaze put her ears flat back and kicked out at him. Mystic nudged again, this time barging his own shoulder against Blaze's rump. The mare kicked out once more and almost caught the gelding, but Mystic stood his ground and Blaze reluctantly gave in and took a step forward... and then another, and another...

Issie grabbed hold of the mare's halter and pulled again. This time Blaze followed her slowly, gingerly stepping out into the muddy paddock towards the stable gate. It seemed to take forever to get there. The storm was getting worse too. Lightning crackled across the sky and the thunder rolled around them as she led Blaze through the gate and into the safety of the stable block.

Issie turned on the stable lights and led Blaze into her stall. Avery had everything ready. The straw had been packed warm and dry underfoot and there was fresh water for Blaze to drink, a hay net and towels and rugs for the mare. Issie grabbed a bundle of towels and began to dry Blaze off. Her first priority was to get her warm and dry. Then she would dash inside and grab Tom and Aidan to help deliver the foal.

Outside Blaze's stable door Issie could hear Mystic nickering and calling as he paced back and forth. The grey pony was anxious – he knew that the foal was coming. Blaze, on the other hand, didn't seem anxious at all. Now that she was inside, the mare seemed quite calm, even taking a nibble from her hay net. Issie had almost got her dried off and was rubbing a towel across Blaze's rump when suddenly the mare tensed up and a gush of water came out from underneath her tail.

Issie froze in fear. She had seen this in the foaling book. Blaze's waters had just broken. The foal was being born! There was no time now to get Tom. She would have to manage this by herself.

"Easy, girl," Issie said, trying to keep herself calm as she stroked Blaze's belly. She quickly grabbed a bandage out of the box in the stall and began to wrap the mare's tail to keep it out of the way.

She had just finished tying the bandage off when Blaze grunted and lay down. As the mare fell sideways on to the soft hay, Issie saw something poking out underneath her tail. She looked closer. There! There was the pale white membrane of the foal sac and a foreleg appearing. Issie watched as, a moment later, another foreleg and then a nose poked out. The foal was coming!

Issie felt the butterflies in her stomach churning. She hadn't finished reading the final chapter on foaling. She had fallen asleep! What was she supposed to do now?

Keep calm, she told herself, *you've read loads of books. You know this. Don't panic.*

As the foal's head emerged further, Issie took a deep breath and pulled herself together. She clasped the two front legs very gently, waited for Blaze to have another contraction and then she pulled downwards. The foal came even further out now, so that its head and shoulders were free. Issie ripped open the foal sac and cleared the foal's nostrils so that it could breathe. Then she stood back as Blaze pushed again. First the foal's tummy then its hindquarters came out, and then there was a sudden glorious rush as the hind legs slid out and the foal landed softly next to Issie on the straw. Issie couldn't believe it. She had done it. She had delivered Blaze's foal!

All three of them – Issie, Blaze and the newborn baby horse – lay there on the floor of the stable for a moment, catching their breath. Then Blaze nickered softly to her baby. The mare grunted, heaving herself slowly up to her feet, and the foal – all wobbly, long, gangly legs – tried to stand with her. At first it tumbled down and fell about on the straw, but eventually it got to its feet and began to drink its first milk.

Blaze licked her foal vigorously, cleaning up its wet coat, and Issie could finally see what her new baby looked like.

The foal was wet but Issie could already see that it was a bay with a black mane and russet body. It had the longest legs Issie had ever seen. It shared the powerful shoulders and haunches of its great sire, Marius. The foal's face, though, had the elegant dish of its dam's Arabian blood and a white blaze, too, just like it's mother.

Issie stroked Blaze's neck. "You did it, Blaze," she said with tears in her eyes as she looked at her beloved horse. "It's a boy. You've got a son."

There was a whinny behind her as Mystic appeared and stuck his head over the Dutch door to see what was going on.

Issie walked over to the grey gelding and hugged him. "It's a colt, Mystic," she whispered to him, "and he's beautiful." She looked at Mystic. "If it hadn't been for you, he wouldn't be here now. Not in weather like this." The little grey seemed agitated. She knew why.

She could hear voices through the noise of the storm. Avery and Aidan were coming.

"Goodbye, Mystic. Thank you, boy," Issie said, burying her face in his mane. Mystic nickered back his goodbye and then spun round and trotted off into the darkness. Issie peered out after him. She could see the glow of two torchlights bobbing about by the house. Avery and Aidan were on their way. Issie had just a few more moments alone with her precious Blaze and her new baby.

She looked at the rain outside the stable doors. The gale had turned even more treacherous now. She watched as the wind bent the trees and the lightning electrified the sky above them. "Born in a night storm," she murmured as she looked over at the little colt...

She had been thinking for months now about what to call Blaze's foal, but nothing had seemed right. Now, as the wind howled around them and the rain fell in sheets, Issie knew what this foal's name was. He was Nightstorm. At that moment, in her heart she knew that one day he would be the greatest horse of them all.

STACY GREGG

PONY CLUB SECRETS

Book Five

Comet and the Champion's Cup

When Aunty Hess opens a riding school for the summer, Issie and her pony-club friends go along to help out. Issie gets to know Comet, a naughty but talented pony with real showjumping promise. But can she train him in time to compete at the Horse of the Year show?

Coming soon!

STACY GREGG

PONY CLUB SECRETS

Book One

Mystic and the Midnight Ride

Issie LOVES horses and is a member of the Chevalier Point
Pony Club, where she looks after her pony Mystic, trains
for gymkhanas and hangs out with her best friends.

When Issie is asked to train Blaze, an abandoned pony,
her riding skills are put to the test. Can she tame the
spirited new horse? And is Blaze really out of danger?

HarperCollins *Children's Books*

STACY GREGG

PONY  CLUB SECRETS

Book Two

Blaze and the Dark Rider

*Issie and her friends have been picked to represent the
Chevalier Point Pony Club at the Interclub Shield – the
biggest competition of the year. It's time to get training!*

*But when equipment is sabotaged and one of the riders
is injured, Issie and her friends are determined to find
out who's to blame...*

HarperCollins *Children's Books*

STACY GREGG

PONY  CLUB SECRETS

Book Three

Destiny and the Wild Horses

Issie goes mad when she finds out she'll be staying with her aunt for the summer. What about the dressage competition she and Blaze have been training so hard for, and her friends at the Chevalier Point Pony Club?

When she finds out Blaze can go with her, and she'll be helping to train movie-star horses, Issie's summer starts to look a whole lot more interesting...

HarperCollins *Children's Books*